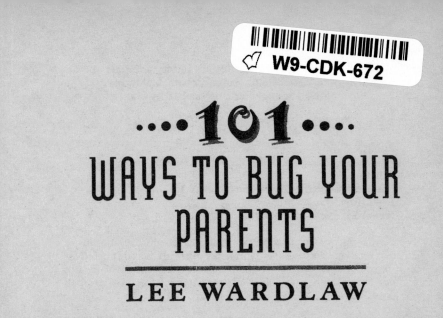

····101····
WAYS TO BUG YOUR PARENTS

LEE WARDLAW

A YEARLING BOOK

Special thanks to Nancy Revlin's third-grade class at
Monte Vista School, Santa Barbara, California,
for dreaming up the original 101 ways.

Published by
Bantam Doubleday Dell Books for Young Readers
a division of
Bantam Doubleday Dell Publishing Group, Inc.
1540 Broadway
New York, New York 10036

Visit us on the Web! www.bdd.com

**Educators and librarians, visit the BDD Teacher's
Resource Center at www.bdd.com/teachers**

ISBN: 0-440-41423-7

Reprinted by arrangement with Dial Books for Young Readers

Printed in the United States of America

July 1998

10 9 8

CWO

For Dian Curtis Regan, who knows
101 ways to make me laugh

ONE

This is it!" I announced to my sixth-grade class. "Stand back!"

Instead everyone crammed closer, peering at my latest invention. It squatted on my desk like a large boxy toad, with a clock for a face and tail-like wires coiling out the back.

"It's *ticking*," Goldie Laux said. "Is it going to explode?" She sounded hopeful.

"No, it's not going to explode."

"I should hope not," said Hiccup Denardo. "I have extremely sensitive ears."

Hiccup is my best friend, personal assistant, and sometimes not-so-willing volunteer. As instructed, he sat forward with his head on the desk, face and shoulders resting just inches from my invention.

"A loud noise could cause partial hearing loss," he warned. "Leading to tinnitus."

"What's toe-night-tus?" Goldie asked. "A foot disease?"

"*Tin-ni-tus*," he corrected. "A condition of the ear

that causes one to hear a buzzing, ringing, roaring, hissing, whistling—"

"There won't be any loud noises," I interrupted. "Because it's *not* a bomb."

"It *looks* like a bomb," Ace stated.

"How would you know?" Goldie demanded.

Ace arced one dark eyebrow. "Believe me," he said in his calm voice. "I know."

An impressed hush fell over the room.

"Wow," someone whispered. "It *must* be a bomb."

I threw up my hands. Not much else I could do. I mean, everyone always believes Ace. That's because he's cool. So cool, he doesn't even have a last name.

"Scribbler left me in charge," Goldie reminded us, "and I say if this is a bomb, he should be here for the detonation. Sneeze, do you want me to get him?"

"Uh, no, that's okay," I said quickly.

Scribbler (real name: Mr. Powell) is our teacher. He'd gone to escort Sugar Schumann to the nurse's office after he (Sugar) ate three platefuls of chocolate-chunk cookies and chugalugged fourteen cups of tropical punch at our last-day-of-school, first-day-of-summer party. I wanted to give my invention a quick test run before the teacher returned.

Last January, after the demonstration of my Christmas Tree Life Extender accidentally melted Scribbler's toupee, he'd forbidden me to bring any of my inventions to school again.

But he couldn't mean *today*. This was a special occasion. As part of the farewell party, Scribbler wanted us to share our summer plans. But I couldn't talk about my invention without anybody actually seeing it. I mean, no one would even believe it worked. Once I proved its success, and Scribbler heard the *ooohs* and *ahhhs* from our class, he'd forgive and forget all the other inventions.

If not? No big deal. In exactly thirty minutes the school year would be over, and I'd never have to see Scribbler again.

"Hey, wait a minute!" Goldie eyed the long wooden spoon attached to one side of the mechanism. Over the spoon part I'd glued a glove, stuffed with marbles to make it stiff. "This *can't* be a bomb," she concluded. "Bombs don't have arms."

"I've been trying to tell you—" I began.

"Well, eef eet eez not a bomb," Pierre Noel said in his phony French accent, "zen vat eez eet?"

Pierre talks like that because he plans to be a world-famous French chef. This might be difficult for two reasons.

One, his mother is a health food nut who never lets him into her herbal-scented, tofu-toting kitchen. She practically washes his mouth out with biodegradable soap if he utters the word *doughnut*.

Two, the only French words Pierre knows are *oui*, which means yes, and *perro*, which he thinks is a fancy kind of bottled water. Actually, it's Spanish for dog, but nobody has the heart to tell him.

"Excuse me," Hiccup said. "Would you mind speeding up the demonstration? This position is extremely uncomfortable. I'm afraid I may develop torticollis."

"Ooo," said Goldie. "Is that a turtle disease?"

He sighed. "*Tor-ti-col-lis:* an illness that affects the fibromuscular tissues of the neck, causing pain, stiffness, and inflammation."

At the word *inflammation* Goldie edged back, as if Hiccup might burst into flames. "Maybe you *should* hurry," she whispered to me.

I nodded. Enough with suspense. Time to wow the class with my brilliance and ingenuity. Time to prove to them at last that I'm more than some runny-nosed nerd.

"Ladies and Gentlemen," I began in a proud voice, "I, Sneeze Wyatt, present to you the latest and greatest in technological feats! The first of its kind! The one and only! The—" I paused for effect—"Nice Alarm!"

"An alarm clock?" Goldie asked. "It's only an *alarm clock*?"

"Vat do we need wis zee alarm clock?" Pierre said. "Eet eez zee last day of school. We do not need to get up for zree whole monthz!"

"Zis, I mean, this is just a model," I said. "It'll take time to have copies made."

"Why is it called the Nice Alarm?" Goldie asked. "Doesn't look very nice to me. Maybe you should paint a smile on it or something."

Pierre snickered. His buddies joined in. They laugh at everything he laughs at, even when it's not funny.

I pretended not to care. A lot of people didn't understand Einstein either.

"It's called the Nice Alarm," I explained patiently, "because it wakes you up *nicely*. Instead of jolting you out of bed with obnoxious buzzing or clanging, this arm lowers and gently taps you twice on the shoulder. Nice, huh?"

"Not bad," Ace said, plucking a thread from his shirt. He's so cool, he probably doesn't even need an alarm clock. Just sets his brain for seven A.M. and BING! Up on time, every time.

I said, "Here, let me demonstrate. Are you ready, Hiccup?"

In answer, my friend started to hic. He does this whenever he's nervous, upset, frightened, stressed, or excited. Which means he hiccups about twenty-three hours a day.

"I'll take that for a yes." I gave his shoulder a reassuring squeeze, then set the Nice Alarm to go off in five seconds.

"Here we go!" I shouted.

Hiccup's hics marched along as the class started a countdown:

"Four! (*hic*)... three! (*hic*)... two! (*hic*)... one! (*hic*)... Blast off!"

Hiccup squeezed his eyes shut.

I held my breath.

Nothing happened.

"What eez zee matter wis eet?" Pierre asked.

"I don't know," I said.

"It really *is* a Nice Alarm," said Goldie. "So nice, it lets you sleep in!"

"No, as Ace say, eet eez a bomb. A failure!" Pierre's buddies cracked up again.

"What's (*hic*) happening?" Hiccup still had his eyes shut.

"Hang in there, pal," I said, reaching for my mini toolbox. "Probably just needs a minor adjustment."

But before I could touch it, the Nice Alarm started to quiver.

And shiver.

And shake.

"Look out!" Goldie cried. "She's going to blow!"

The Nice Alarm chittered across the desk.

Then the arm swooped down and karate-chopped Hiccup on the nose.

TWO

"By doze!" Hiccup howled, cupping his hands over the middle of his face. "It boke by doze!"

"Sorry!" I cried. "Move your hands a sec. Let me see."

Goldie skirted toward the door. "I'll get my mother, the Vice-Principal!" she called. (Goldie reminds us fifty times a day that her mother is Vice-Principal.)

"Wait . . . don't!" I pictured the V. P. making me stay after school on the last day.

Or worse, making me repeat sixth grade with Scribbler.

I shuddered. Better take my punishment *now*.

"Get Scribbler!" I said. "And some ice!"

Goldie nodded and raced out the door.

"Should we call 9-1-1?" someone asked.

"Maybe you should invent a backup alarm that gives CPR," Ace suggested.

"He'll be okay," I insisted, but my voice wobbled. "Hiccup, let me see your doze. I mean, nose." I tugged at his hands.

"Is it breeding?" he asked.

"No, it's not bleeding. Just a little red, that's all."

"Great going, Sneeze," Ace said with a yawn. "You've given your best friend a concussion. Wonder what you do to your enemies?"

I winced. "But I didn't *mean* to hurt him!" How could anyone think I'd do this on purpose? Not only is Hiccup my best friend, he's my *only* friend.

I patted his back. "Honest, pal, it was an accident."

"Oui, like all your inventions," said Pierre. "Remembare zee Glow-in-zee-Dark Toilet Seat? Zee one zat give Scribbler zee glow-in-zee-dark butt?"

"That was a great idea," I defended. "It would've saved millions of people from stumbling over things at night while trying to find the bathroom. The invention just has a few bugs to be worked out."

"Did you say *bugs*," Ace asked, "or *butts*?"

"And what about the bubble gum you invented?" someone else challenged. "The kind that wasn't supposed to lose its flavor."

"I remembare," Pierre said. "Eet turn zee teeth blue!"

More laughter. My cheeks flushed hot.

Just then Scribbler and Goldie hurried in.

"Show's over, people," our teacher said. "Take your seats, please. Mr. Denardo, let me see that nose of yours."

Hiccup has so many freckles splattered over his face, Scribbler probably couldn't even *find* his nose.

I'm lucky. I have only nineteen freckles. If you connect the dots with a pen, it looks like a picture of the space shuttle flying toward my left ear.

"That smarts, I bet," Scribbler told Hiccup sympathetically, "but it doesn't seem to be broken. A little swollen, maybe. Miss Laux, did you bring the ice cubes?"

She nodded. "I found the ones Pierre's mother made for our tropical punch. They're frozen into the shape of endangered animals."

"Uh, very nice," Scribbler said, his lips twitching. He edged toward the third drawer of his desk, where he keeps his special notepad and pen.

Goldie found out by spying—her mission in life— on her mother-the-Vice-Principal that our teacher is writing a book. Every time one of us says or does something that makes his lips twitch, he scribbles it into his notepad. Which is why Ace, who nicknamed all of us, dubbed him Scribbler.

I suspect his book must be about our class. All I can say is, if he mentions any of my inventions, he'd better dedicate the book to me.

"What kind of ice cubes do you want?" Goldie was asking Hiccup. "California condor? Spotted owl?"

It didn't seem to make much difference. They were all going to melt into extinction in a few minutes anyway.

Without waiting for an answer, she wrapped a few

cubes in a towel. "You're supposed to hold this against your nose."

"Is that towel cotton or polyester?" Hiccup asked. "Synthetic fibers cause me to experience allergic rhinitis."

"Is that a rhino disease?" Goldie asked.

"No, it's a symptom complex that—"

"Mr. Denardo," Scribbler interrupted, "do you need to see the nurse?"

My friend shook his towel-head.

"Good. Then I'd like to hear everyone's summer plans." Scribbler picked up the Nice Alarm. Holding it at arm's length, he moved it to his desk. Then he dusted off his hands as though my invention were dirty.

"You," he said to me with a frown in his voice. "After class. Let's talk."

I gulped and nodded.

"Don't worry," Hiccup whispered. "I'll stay and vouch for you."

What a pal. True blue. Actually, thanks to me, true black-and-blue.

"Summer plans," Scribbler said. "Who wants to go first?"

Goldie waved her arm as if she was doing the hula.

"Yes, Miss Laux?"

"My mother, the Vice-Principal, is taking me to Hollywood. We're going on a bus tour of movie stars' homes. And we have tickets to see the new talk show *Gossip Gourmet.*"

Scribbler cleared his throat. "Sounds, uh, educational."

Goldie's an A1 gossip. Her real name is Trudy, but Ace nicknamed her in honor of that snoopy storybook girl, Goldilocks. You don't dare tell your best friend a secret without first checking to see if Goldie is eavesdropping. Even if you're in the boys' bathroom.

"Ace, how about you?" Scribbler asked. "What do you plan to do this summer?"

Ace shrugged. "Hang out."

"Hang out where?"

"Nowhere."

"How long will you be there?"

Another shrug. "As long as it takes."

Scribbler shot a twitching glance toward his desk drawer and sighed. "Anyone else?"

Pierre wanted to sign up for a French cooking class.

Tiny Ramirez was going to Mexico to visit her grandmother.

Sinking Sam planned to take Beginning Swimming at the municipal pool (for the third summer in a row).

"I've got four doctors' appointments scheduled," Hiccup said when his turn came. His voice warmed with anticipation. "I think I might have gastroenteritis. Or gallstones. Maybe even Goodpasture's syndrome."

"Is that a cow disease?" asked Goldie.

I nudged my friend. "Hey, you forgot to mention you're going on vacation with *me*."

"Yes, that's correct," Hiccup said. "Sneeze and his parents have invited me to northern California for a month. We plan to engage in many outdoor activities, such as boating, fishing, and hiking. All that fresh air is beneficial to Sneeze's allergies. You do know he has allergies, don't you?"

The class groaned. How could they *not* know? Especially after I sneezed 147 times the first day of kindergarten. (That's why Ace exchanged my real name, Steve, for you-know-what.) We live in southern California, which means there's a lot for me to be allergic to. If it grows, blooms, purrs, barks, burrows, flies, or belches out of the back of a car, I'll sneeze at it.

"Anything you'd like to add about the trip, Mr. Wyatt?" Scribbler asked.

"Well," I began, "the best part is we're spending three whole days in San Francisco at a—"

"I-don't-think-so," Goldie sang under her breath.

I half turned. "What?"

She only smiled, so I went on. "As I was saying, we're going to San Francisco for the Invention Convention. Inventors from all over the country will be there and I'm taking..."

I stopped. Suddenly it didn't seem like a good idea to remind Scribbler of the I-word.

I gave a little cough. "And, um, yeah. Like Hiccup said. We plan to fish and stuff."

"I-don't-think-so," Goldie hummed again.

"Sounds relaxing, Mr. Wyatt," Scribbler said. "Who else wants to share?"

I turned to face Goldie. "*What* don't you think so?" I whispered.

"Oh, one overhears things. Things that no one else knows, except one's mother, the Vice-Principal."

My stomach cringed. "What things?" I demanded. "What are you talking about?"

"You'll find out soon enough."

"Goldie—"

"I can't say any more. I might get into trouble."

"*Goldie—*"

"Okay, okay, I'll tell you. But you'll owe me, and you'll owe me big."

"No way. I'm broke. I spent next year's allowance on the Nice Alarm."

Goldie swooped a hunk of blond hair over her shoulder. "I don't want money. I want...*information*."

The word sent cold worm-slithers down my neck.

I peeked to see if Scribbler had noticed us talking, then lowered my whisper. "What kind of information?"

"I'll tell you when the time comes," she replied.

"Couldn't I just name one of my inventions after you? How about the Goldie Alarm?"

She made a face. "Right. Like I really want to be known for a nose amputation machine."

"Okay. I'll get you your . . . information. Now spill it."

Goldie leaned so close, our noses almost touched. She whispered, "You think this is the last day of school, but it's not. At least not for you. In a way, it's kind of the *first* day of school."

"What are you talking about? You're crazy." I started to turn away.

"This is serious!" Goldie hissed. "You think you're going on vacation? You think you're going to some stupid convention? Well, you're not!"

"Oh, yeah?" I tried to sound tough, but those worm-slithers had returned. "And just where am I going instead?"

Goldie smiled. A smug I-told-you-so smile. "You," she announced, "are going to summer school!"

THREE

The bell rang.

A great *YAHOO!* burst open like a parachute over the room.

"School's out!" I cried, high-five-ing Hiccup. "Let's go!"

Goldie clutched my sleeve. "But, I was just about to tell you—"

"Good-bye, Goldie, good-bye!" I cried, pulling away. Those worm-slithers I'd felt had slunk into a dark corner of my mind. "You can tell me in junior high. *If* you're lucky. C'mon, Hic!"

We grabbed our things and sprinted to the door. Outside, chaos ruled. Cars honked. Buses sputtered. Kids raced around shrieking and laughing, trailing sweaters, books, papers, report cards, and pungent tuna-fish sandwiches that had been stashed in lockers since Halloween.

"Excuse me, Sneeze," Hiccup said. "I don't mean to suggest that you're suffering from amnesia, but have you forgotten that Scribbler wished to speak with you after school?"

Rats. I *had* forgotten.

"I can't go back now. We'll miss our bus to town." I pushed through a knot of kids. "Besides, all Scribbler's gonna do is yell at me about bringing the Nice Alarm and..."

I froze. "The Alarm!" I shouted. "It's still on Scribbler's desk! Wait for me!"

I raced back to the room. Goldie was buried in her own desk, whisking out old papers and tossing them behind her. She looked like a dog digging a hole in the sand.

Scribbler stood across the room, lecturing Ace about his dried bubble gum sculpture of the Principal's profile, which Scribbler had found under a desk.

"But she looks so pretty in pink," Ace was explaining.

"I can't find my Elvis stamps!" Goldie wailed.

Nobody noticed me.

Now was my chance.

I edged into the room. Sidled up to Scribbler's desk. My fingers inched toward the Nice Alarm.

And then—it happened.

My nose started to tickle.

And tingle.

And itch.

I tried to hold back the sneeze. Really I did. But I had only two choices: Burst my eardrums, or let 'er rip.

"*Ahhh*-CHOOEY!"

Goldie's head popped up. "Sneeze! You're back! I'm glad you came to your senses. Listen, we *have* to talk."

"Mr. Wyatt," Scribbler broke in. "Don't we have an appointment? I'll be with you in just a moment."

"Uh, um, sorry, folks," I said, easing the Nice Alarm into my pack. "I'd love to stay and chat, but, uh, gotta go. Bye!"

I shot out the door.

"Sneeze!" Goldie called after me.

"Mis-ter Wy-att!" Scribbler yelled.

"Incoming!" I cried as I met up with Hiccup. I dragged him toward our bus that was idling at the curb. I charged up the steps and leaped into the nearest seat.

"Would you mind (*hic*) shutting that window?" Hiccup asked. "The carbon monoxide (*hic-hic*) gives me vertigo and dyspnea."

"In a second," I said, slouching low. "If Scribbler comes out, I don't want him to see me. Get down!"

"You can't disobey a teacher like that," Hiccup warned. "There could be serious re(*hic*)percussions."

"Get a grip, Hic. Our elementary-school lives are over. We're never gonna see Scribbler again. *If* this bus would only start moving. Now, take a deep breath, hold it, and count to ten."

"Not until you shut the window," he insisted. "Carbon monoxide poisoning can also cause confusion, convulsions, coma—"

"Okay, okay," I said, slamming the window closed.

With grinding gears, the bus finally grunted and lurched toward town. I sighed and patted the Nice Alarm through my pack. We were safe. Free of Scribbler now and forever.

"No, no, no, no, *no*," said Regan, owner of the Tool Box, the instant Hiccup and I walked in the door.

The Tool Box is the hardware store where I get all the supplies for my inventions. I stop there every day after school, even if I don't need to buy anything.

I like to walk up and down the aisles, dipping my hands into cold bin after bin, listening to the clink-clank of nuts, bolts, plugs, washers, and rivets as they cascade through my fingers. The store has pea-soup-green linoleum floors and fluorescent lights that turn your skin the same color. But the air has a good oily, metallic smell. The smell of screwdrivers and wrenches, hammers and drills. The smell of inventions to come.

"No, no, *no*," Regan repeated. He made a cross with his fingers like you do when warding off vampires.

"Have I asked for anything?" I said innocently, stepping up to the counter. "Maybe Hiccup and I just came in to graze."

"Grazing's for cows," Regan replied. "You mean browse. And don't try to change the subject! I recognize that look. That's your I-spent-all-my-allowance-

and-need-a-couple-of-freebies look. Am I right? Well, the answer is no."

He tucked in his grease-smudged T-shirt, trying to look more managerial, I guess. The shirt read: When It Comes to Nuts and Bolts We Don't Screw Around.

"I'm not looking for freebies," I said. "Honest. But I do need a couple of parts, and I was kinda hoping we could start a tab."

"A tab? A *tab*? This isn't a bar, kiddo. It's a business. And to stay in business I've got to *sell* things. You know, like, for money? Dough? Moola? Dinero?"

"I appreciate that," I said. "Really, I do. But look, something's wrong with the Nice Alarm, and I'm not sure what. And I've *got* to get it fixed before the Convention. It's a matter of life and death."

I unzipped my pack, easing out the Alarm. "Couldn't you just take a peek? Please?"

I had him. Regan's an inventor too. He goes to the Convention every year, and can't resist a puzzle. He snatched the Alarm out of my hands, peering at it with brow-wrinkling concentration. "What's the problem?"

"Its current mission is to seek out and destroy all living noses," Hiccup answered.

"What?"

"The arm is whapping instead of tapping," I explained.

"Hmmm." Regan unhitched the back cover. "Well,

no wonder! You've got a pull spring in here. That's why the arm has no control. Easy as nachos to fix. You just need a compression spring, socket head cap-screw, and a hex key to drive it. Regular screwdriver won't work."

"Uh, how much will all that cost?"

"Oh, about ten bucks."

I winced. "The other problem is that I—"

"Don't have ten bucks," Regan finished for me.

I nodded.

He sighed. "Let me check in the back. Maybe I can find a couple of discontinued parts I can let you have at a discount." He lumbered through a door marked Employees Only.

"I'd be more than happy to loan you the ten dollars," Hiccup offered.

I shook my head. "Thanks, but I know you've been saving for years to buy that classic Superman comic."

Hiccup collects comic books. In fact, he's been drawing a series of his own about a superhero named Medicine Man. With his red hair and freckles, M.M. (as Medicine Man is called) kind of resembles Hiccup—*if* he inflated his muscles to pumpkin size with a bicycle pump.

M.M. wears purple tights and a green cape that flaps proudly in the breeze when he flies through the air making house calls. "I'm here to wipe out the disease of injustice!" M.M. booms as he slaps criminals in the face with a stethoscope and prescribes aspirin and plenty of liquids for the victims.

"I don't mind," Hiccup was saying. "It's the least I can do to repay your parents for taking me on vacation. That is, if we're still *going* on vacation."

Goldie's words echoed in my mind: *You think you're going to some stupid convention? Well, you're not. You're going to summer school!*

I shuddered. Then I shoved her words off a mental cliff.

"Of course we're still going on vacation. No way would we cancel. We haven't gone away in five years—not since Dad started working on his Ph.D.—and we've been planning this trip for months. Goldie must've spent too many hours with her ear pressed against doors. She's got splinters in her brain."

Hiccup nodded. "That type of injury would explain much about her personality."

"Besides," I said, lowering my voice, "we *have* to go. Someone's expecting me at the Convention. Someone important." Gingerly I pulled from my pack a letter I'd received the day before. "Are your hands clean? Okay, take a look at this. Wait—first you have to promise not to breathe a word of the contents to anyone. Especially my parents. I want this to be a surprise. Swear?"

Hiccup put a hand over his heart. "I swear on the honor of M.M."

I nodded, then placed the envelope into his palm like it was the June 1938 *Action Comics* Number One he'd been saving for.

As Hiccup read, I closed my eyes. I could picture the bold, gold letterhead and the sharp, slanty lines of the signature. And I'd memorized every sentence, every word:

PATTERSON ENTERPRISES, INC.
PITTSBURGH, PENNSYLVANIA

To: Stephen J. Wyatt, President
I'VE GOT AN IDEA, INC.

Re: "The Nice Alarm"

Dear Mr. Wyatt:

Thank you for your letter of May 17th. I have reviewed your plans and description of the Nice Alarm and find it a most intriguing idea.

I would like to meet with you to discuss the possibility of purchasing, manufacturing, and distributing this novelty product.

I have set up an appointment for you at the Patterson Enterprises booth, #1738, at 2:00 P.M., July 26th. I hope this will be convenient. My schedule is quite full, and this will be my only free time slot.

22

I look forward to meeting you.

Sincerely,

Sterling Patterson
Sterling Patterson, President
Patterson Enterprises, Inc.

"Wow!" Hiccup said. "(*hic-hic*) Wow!"

A giddy laugh bubbled up from my chest. "Yeah, I know." I refolded the letter and tucked it back into my pack. Then I scurried to the watercooler and filled a paper cup. "Here, drink this."

He took a few gulps. "I was not aware your middle initial is J."

"It's not. I don't have a middle name. I just thought the J looked impressive."

"And what's this 'I've Got an Idea, (*hic*) Inc'?"

"Oh, that's my invention company."

"I didn't know you had—"

"I don't," I interrupted. "But you don't think this Mr. Patterson would want to meet me if he knew I was a *kid*, do you? Anyway, I couldn't take the risk. This is my big chance to make my dream come true. My chance to show everybody—Scribbler, Goldie, Pierre, *everybody*—that I'm not just a wad of used tissue."

I gazed out at my future looming bright on the horizon. "Think of it, Hiccup. People will *like* me.

They'll wanna hang out with me, be friends with me. And I'll be famous. Rich and famous. I'll be on talk shows. On the covers of magazines. And—"

"*I* like you," Hiccup put in.

Regan reappeared. He smacked a small box onto the counter.

"Here's what I'm gonna do, kiddo. I'll let you have the compression spring, the hex key, *and* the cap-screw for six eighty-nine. That's my best offer. Take it or leave it."

I dug into my jeans pocket. "Well, here's the nine," I said, counting out pennies. "And I can have the six-eighty for you by—"

"Monday," Regan said, his voice firm.

"Where am I gonna get that much money in three days?" I asked.

"Try that old miniature golf place. What's it called?" Regan thought a minute, scratching his arm near the tattoo of a screwdriver. "Gadabout Golf, that's it! Go fish balls out of the pond. They pay twenty-five cents apiece for 'em. No wonder they're going bankrupt."

"I don't know," I said. "That counter girl is always squinting her eyes at me, like I'm gonna try to smuggle out a golf club up my sleeve."

Regan closed his hand over the box. "Look, I've got to make *some* profit here. I'm saving for the Invention

Convention, and it's not cheap. So, like I said, this is my best offer. Take it or leave it."

"I'll take it." I tugged at the box till he finally let go.

Hiccup and I hurried outside before Regan could change his mind. Hic blinked at the bright sun. "It's probably best I do not accompany you to Gadabout Golf tomorrow," he said. "The weather channel forecasts hotter temperatures and I'm all out of sunscreen. I believe I'm getting a basal-cell carcinoma."

"A what?"

"Skin cancer. Right here." He pointed under his left eye.

"That's a freckle," I said. "Besides, we've got plenty of sunscreen at our house. And I'll loan you a baseball cap. How about the one from the medical center? The one my mom gave me?"

Hiccup's eyes flashed a glazed doughnut look. He's got a big crush on Mom. She's a microbiologist and the only person who understands him when he starts tossing around words like *botulism* and *staphylococcus*.

"Well ..." he said.

"If you want to stay home, I'll understand," I went on. "But I could really use your help. Please? For the Nice Alarm?"

"Well ..."

"I wonder what M.M. would do at a time like this?"

I said casually. "I'll bet *he* wouldn't let a little basal-cell whatever stop him from coming to the rescue of a friend."

Hiccup straightened, shoulders back, chin raised. I could almost imagine a cape fluttering in the breeze behind him. "You're absolutely correct. Tomorrow we shall press onward to Gadabout Golf. Nine A.M. Sharp!"

FOUR

Mom—I'm home!" I called, unlocking the back door. "See ya tomorrow, Hic. Let's ride our bikes to Gadabout, okay?"

My friend didn't answer. Instead he craned his neck to gaze into the house, hoping to catch a glimpse of Mom, I guessed.

I wiped the sweat off my forehead. Even though it was after five, the sun still blazed so hot I could almost feel my hair singeing. Maybe I could invent a baseball cap that came with a mini sprinkler on top. It would connect to a little battery-powered water pump hidden in a shirt pocket and ...

I started to draw the plans in my mind. Then I noticed Hiccup still standing there. He sighed. "I know it's improper to invite one's self for dinner," he said, "but ... may I *please* stay for dinner?"

"I don't know. You've already eaten at our house four times this week. Not including breakfast this morning."

Hiccup's family has six boys and eight dogs, so he doesn't get much attention at home. I wonder if that's why he's sick all the time—just trying to get some-body to notice him. Might be easier if he learned how to bark.

"Besides," I continued, "this is pizza night. And you've got that cheese disorder."

"It's called lactose intolerance," Hiccup corrected, "and it's not the cheese that my stomach can't toler-ate, but the milk sugar found in cheese that—"

I interrupted by sneezing eight times in a row.

"Let's get you inside," Hiccup fussed. He pushed me into the house and slammed the door.

I set the Nice Alarm on the kitchen table, slung my backpack onto a chair, blew my nose, then took a few cool gulps of allergy-free air-conditioning. "Ahh, that's better. *Mom!*"

The only answer was a soft tip...tip...tip.

Rats. My E-Z Chocolate Milk Dispenser was leak-ing again.

I rigged our refrigerator so you can get milk and chocolate syrup from the water and ice dispensers. Only problem is, I haven't figured out how to regulate the temperature of the chocolate. It either freezes into brown icicles or dribbles into sludge puddles on the floor. The puddles mean everything else in the freezer is defrosting too.

"Do you want a snack?" I asked as I swiped at the puddle with a paper towel. "Help yourself to chocolate milk. Or there are probably a few formerly frozen TV dinners in there."

Hiccup opened the freezer and wrinkled his nose. "Thank you, no. The last time I ate a TV dinner, I thought it gave me shingles."

"Is that a roof disease?" I asked, mimicking Goldie.

"No, it's a virus that—"

The phone rang.

Hiccup lunged for it. "Maybe it's *her*." He sounded dream-come-true-ish.

I snatched the receiver from his hands.

"Hello, sweetheart." Mom's voice bubbled like soda pop over the line.

I pushed the speaker button so Hiccup could hear her too.

"Where are you?" I asked.

"Still at the lab."

I pictured her dressed in a white lab coat, the phone crooked between shoulder and chin, one eye peering into her microscope at swimming bacteria.

"I'm finishing up my last experiment for the day," she went on, "and then I'll head home. One hour, tops."

"Is that one hour real time or Mom time?" I asked. Research and experiments always take longer than they're supposed to. So if Mom says one hour, sometimes she really means the day after tomorrow.

"One hour *real* time," Mom insisted, as if she'd never been late in her whole life. She forgets she almost gave birth to me in an elevator because she waited too long for test results on a lab rabbit. The rabbit's name was Steve, which ended up on my birth certificate. I should be grateful his name wasn't Peter Cottontail.

"I forgot to get something out for dinner," Mom went on. "I want to make your favorite. Fajitas. Would you mind defrosting a chicken in the microwave?"

I glanced at the freezer, from which Hiccup had just removed a plastic bag full of chicken parts. "Uh, already taken care of. Hey, wait a minute, it's pizza night!"

"I want to make a special dinner for you, dear. Dad and I need to talk with you about, um . . . our summer plans."

Something in Mom's voice made my ears itch with suspicion. She'd used that same tone one night last year, when she said, "Dad and I need to talk with you about your tonsils." Two days later a doctor carved them out with a chain saw.

Okay, so he didn't really use a chain saw, but it sure felt that way.

Come to think of it, Mom hadn't made fajitas since the night she told me about my surgery. . . .

"Hiccup and I want to talk about our summer plans too," I said, rubbing the goose bumps that had appeared on my arm. "Like, when do we leave? How long is the drive? Where are we staying during the Convention?"

"Hmmm?" Mom said, suddenly distracted. The bugs under her scope must've started the backstroke. "Oh, um, we'll talk about everything at dinner. And if Hiccup's there, please send him home. I think this should be a private family discussion. Gotta run—my timer just went off." She hung up. Mom never remembers to say good-bye.

"Something is wrong, Hic," I said, replacing the receiver. "Very wrong. No matter what happens, you are definitely staying for dinner. No way will Mom and Dad dare to break bad news if there's a guest in the house."

"Perhaps I could spend the weekend," he suggested.

"Sure. Let's go to my room."

Upstairs Hiccup settled onto my bed with his sketches for the latest adventures of M.M. As he proofread the pages, I sprinkled food flakes into my aquarium. (Fish are the only kind of pets I'm not allergic to.) Alexander Graham Bell, Edison, and the Wright Brothers darted to the surface, slurping flakes like marine vacuum cleaners. But Lipman (named after the guy who invented the first pencil with attached eraser) hovered near the bottom, just staring at me. With his pale pop-eyes and ceaselessly moving mouth, he reminded me of Goldie.

As if Hiccup had read my mind, he said, "I perceive that you're beginning to believe her. About summer school, I mean."

I whirled to face him. "But it doesn't make sense! Why would I have to go to summer school? I haven't flunked any classes. I'm a straight-A student."

"Then you have nothing to fear," he replied. "Unless, of course, your father flunks the fish test."

The fish test.

My stomach flipped. Whenever Dad feels guilty about something, he brings home a new tropical fish for my aquarium. He brought Lipman when Mom had to work during my twelfth birthday party. Edison showed up the weekend Dad canceled our Disneyland trip because he was taking exams. And Bell—

"I don't want to talk about the fish test," I said. "I don't want to talk about any tests. School is over. Period. I'm not going back until September, even if Dad walks in here with Moby Dick. Now, if you'll excuse me, I need to get to work on the Nice Alarm."

A car pulled into the drive. I froze in my desk chair, afraid to look out the window.

I heard jangling keys. The front door opening. Footsteps coming up the stairs. A knock on my door.

"Steve? You in there?"

Dad's voice. Dad's knock.

I gulped. "Yeah, I'm here." My voice sounded rusty.

32

"Come in, Dad."

He entered wearing his usual rumpled suit, rumpled hair, and rumpled smile. Dad's a part-time professor at three community colleges. He claims he spends more time rushing from one campus to the other than he does in the classroom. Dad always drives his 1976 Cadillac convertible with the top down—which is probably why he always looks so rumpled.

"Hello, Son," he said cheerily. "Ah, hello again, Hiccup. It's been a desert these ten hours since we last set eyes upon each other." He winked at me. That's when I noticed he held one hand behind his back. "I brought you a present, Steve. I—"

"No!" I leapt to my feet. Knocked over my chair. "No presents! Don't need 'em. Don't want 'em. Thanks anyway, Dad. And thanks for stopping by. Really. It's been great. See you at dinner, okay?"

Dad gave a nervous laugh. "What's gotten into you? You love presents. And you'll love this one. Trust me. It's soothing to watch. Easy-care. Doesn't eat much. And doesn't make you sneeze. It's—"

"A fish," said Hiccup.

"Well, yes," Dad said, sounding surprised. He held out a plastic bag filled with water. Inside swirled a Lipman look-alike.

That's when my brain snapped.

"*Aaaaaarrrgggghh!*" I cried. I raced around the

room, arms flailing, like a bratty four-year-old. "You can't cancel our vacation! You can't send me to summer school! I won't go, I won't, I won't!"

"Who told you about summer school?" Dad asked.

"Who *cares* who told me! I only care if it's true. Is it? *Is it?*"

He sighed. "Yes, I'm afraid it is."

"Aaaaaarrrgggghh!"

"Now, calm down." Dad, still holding the plastic bag, was waving his arms too. The fish sloshed around like it was in the middle of a hurricane. "Let's sit and have a nice, quiet discussion."

"It's not a discussion if I don't have a say," I yelled. "You and Mom already made all the decisions, so what's the point? I refuse to listen anymore." I stuffed my fingers in my ears and started to hum. Loudly.

"Son, let me explain. Your mother's research is not going well. There's just no way she can take off for a whole month and—"

"LA-DEE-DA-DEE-DA," I sang. "I-CAN'T-HEAR-A-WORD!"

"—and we can't afford it now either," Dad went on. "With school cutbacks, I've lost two of my fall positions. I have to teach summer school to—"

"DOO-BEE-DOO-BEE-DOO," I warbled.

"Steve, stop it!"

"BOH-DEE-OH-DOH—"

"Steve!"

"HIC!" hiccupped Hiccup. "HIC! HIC-HIC!"

It was the worse case of hiccups I'd ever heard. They burst out fast and furious, like popcorn sputtering in a hot saucepan.

"Hey, are you okay?" I asked.

"HIC-HIC-HIC!" he answered. His face turned red.

"Do something, Dad! He's gonna explode!"

"Get some water," Dad ordered. "And a paper bag—quick!"

I flew down to the kitchen and back. "Here!"

Dad took the glass of water and put it to Hiccup's mouth. "Try a few sips," he urged.

"HIC-GULP!" said Hiccup. "HIC-GULP-HIC!"

"It's not working!"

"Okay, okay. Let's try this." Dad held the paper bag over Hiccup's nose and mouth. "Just breathe deep and slow. That's it."

"HIC! HIC-CUP!"

"Maybe we should stand him on his head," I shouted over the hics. "Honest, I read somewhere that it really works."

"Worth a try. Bottoms up!" Dad hoisted my friend by the ankles.

"HIC-WHUP!" said Hiccup.

The top of his head brushed the carpet. I bent down, covering his nose and mouth again with the paper bag. "Okay, breathe *slowly*."

"HIC-HIC-HIC-HIC!"

"What on earth is going on in here?!"

Mom stood in the doorway, her forehead wrinkled with confusion and worry. Rays from the setting sun streamed through the window, framing her in a halo.

"HIC-*ahhhhh*," said Hiccup. He gazed at her with upside-down adoration.

Doctors might laugh. Scientists might scoff. No one outside my room might ever believe it. But that day, my friend discovered a cure for hiccups: the beautiful face of my mother.

If only I could find a quick and painless cure for *my* problem.

FIVE

*T*hings to Do to Bug Mom and Dad

1. Give them the silent treatment.
2. Leave wads of used Kleenex all over the house. Soggy wads.
3. Sigh a lot.
4. Invite Hiccup to live with us.
5. Never help carry groceries again.
6. Never change my underwear again.
7. ?

After dinner I sat at my desk, making a list and checking it twice. I'd finished repairing the Nice Alarm and knew I should test it. But if I wasn't going to the Convention, what was the point? I mean, I'm only a twelve-year-old kid. My parents are older than me. *Bigger* than me. They have all the money and all the clout. So if they say the vacation is canceled, there's nothing I can do about it.

Except bug them until they go out of their minds.

Or until they *change* their minds.

"Steve!" Mom called from downstairs. "Would you *please* come fix your Chocolate Milk Dispenser? It's leaking all over the floor!"

"In a minute," I called back.

"That's what you said *twenty* minutes ago!"

"Yeah, well, I'm busy. I'll be there in a minute!"

Mom made a noise like a cow giving birth, which is her way of saying *you're really starting to irritate me, Steve*.

I smiled. Then I erased the question mark next to number seven and wrote:

Tell them I'll do something in a minute. Then never do it.

My aquarium chuckled beside me. I peered into the tank, watching my new fish, Benedict Arnold, swim through the bubbles.

"Hey, Ben," I said. "You must think The List is devious. Heartless. Mean. Yeah, well, you're right. But Mom and Dad didn't exactly act like Santa Claus tonight."

My thoughts dragged back to our dinner conversation, after they sent the dehiccupped Hiccup home....

"You seem to think we've canceled this vacation just to torture you," Dad had said. "And that's not true. We know the trip is important to you. It's important to all of us. But money is tight right now. And so is time."

I stabbed at a tortilla with my fork. "But this *always* happens. We never go anywhere. *Never!*"

"We'll make it up to you," Mom said. "I promise. We'll try to get away for a few days at Christmas."

"Is that Christmas real time?" I asked. "Or Mom time? Like, Christmas in the twenty-third century?"

She huffed into her fajita. "It doesn't help to be sarcastic, dear."

"But Christmas will be too late!"

"Do we have any salsa?" Dad asked, shuffling things in the refrigerator. He pulled out a small glass container lined with red stuff. "Ah, here it is!"

"Don't eat that!" Mom cried. "That's a petri dish. I've got an experiment growing in there!"

Dad shuddered. He eased the dish to a far corner of the fridge, then grabbed a bottle of ketchup.

"Is anybody listening to me?" I asked. "We have to go away this summer. We have to go to the Invention Convention. I can't tell you why, but my career as an inventor depends on it! Couldn't we drive up to San Francisco for just a few days?"

"The Convention is one reason why we have to cancel," Dad explained, splotching ketchup onto his fajita. "It's terribly expensive. We can't afford it right now."

"Two days," I begged. "Just two teeny-weeny little days. That's all I ask. That's all I need."

"Steve—" Mom began.

"Dad, we could take the *convertible*." I dangled the word like a worm on a hook. "Picture it: driving up the coast. Top down, sun glinting off the hood. The wind in your hair, the salt air tickling your nose..."

For a moment Dad gazed across the kitchen, hands gripping his fajita like a steering wheel. Then he ran my illusion off the road.

"I'm sorry, Son," he said. "It's tempting, but we can't."

I heaved a huge sigh. "I guess you two don't want me to grow up to be a world-renowned inventor. I guess I'd better start filling out that application to Sanitation Services School."

Mom pursed her lips. I love to bug her with this comment. She's been worried about my future ever since the day she caught me, at age three, holed up inside of the kitchen trash can. Wearing hamburger on my T-shirt, orange peel earrings, and a coffee filter hat, I announced: *Ste-vie wan-na be a gah-bage man!*

"Do you think we students will get extra credit if we bring our own garbage?" I asked. "I could start my collection right now." I moved to scrape the uneaten dinner off my plate and into the trash.

"Sit down," Mom ordered, pointing her fork at me. "And please stop all that garbageman garbage. You're going to college. And then to graduate school. And then—"

"*School!*" I pronounced the word as if it tasted like cat food. "It's bad enough you're canceling the vacation. Why do I have to go to summer school? Why can't I stay home and work on my inventions?"

"Your mother and I don't feel comfortable leaving you here alone all day," Dad said. "Especially after what happened last summer. Remember when you tried your Super-Duper Stain Remover on the living room sofa?"

"Hey, it made the stain disappear, didn't it?" I asked.

He nodded. "And the sofa cushion, and the sofa springs, and a three-foot section of carpet *underneath* the sofa—"

"What about something fun," I broke in, "like camp?"

"All the activities we checked on are either too expensive or already filled for the summer," Mom said. "Besides, the class we signed you up for *is* fun. And it's only three hours a day. Hiccup will be in it too, so you can go home with him at noon. Wait a minute, where did I put that brochure?"

She leapt up and started rummaging through the junk drawer. Then her briefcase. Then her purse.

I slumped low in my chair. "Dad," I pleaded, "please tell me I'm signed up for an inventing class."

He coughed. "Well, *er*, not exactly. But the class does require an inventive mind. Say, how's that new fish of yours doing? Do you think he'd like another swimmate?"

"Oh, here it is!" Mom said. She dug a crumpled

sheet from the bottom of her lab coat pocket and began to read aloud:

Recipe for a Book
A Class for Young Authors

Setting Up:
Student writers will learn tasty tips for creating and mixing essential ingredients needed to bake a delicious book.

"*What?!*" My voice squeaked. "It's a *writing* class? Let me see that!"

I whisked the pamphlet from her hands and tried to smooth out the wrinkles. Even then I couldn't believe what I was reading:

Appetizers:
The class features a menu of writing workshops and lectures by guest authors, poets, and storytellers, plus mouth-watering field trips to a printing press and a local publishing house.

Main Course:
Working alone or in small groups, student chefs will write, illustrate, and bind their own fiction, nonfiction, or poetry books.

Dessert:
All books will be displayed at the public library during the countywide celebration of Young Authors' Month in Au-

gust. Awards will be presented to the best books submitted. Bon appétit!

The pamphlet slipped from my fingers. "I *hate* writing," I said. "You know that. *Why* did you sign me up for a stupid writing class?"

"Well, um..." Dad ran a hand through his rumpled hair, "it was the only class that still had openings."

"No wonder!" I wadded up my napkin and slam-dunked it onto my plate. "The class sounds corny. Full of baloney. The description alone gives me indigestion." I shoved back my chair.

"Where are you going?" Mom asked. "We haven't finished our dinner."

"Excuse me," I answered, "but I need to drink a Pepto-Bismol milkshake—extra, extra thick." Then I stomped from the room.

"...and that's the whole horrible story, Ben," I said.

Benedict Arnold didn't say anything. Fish never do. Which is why I like them. They're excellent listeners. They don't boss you around.

And they never break promises.

"How could they do this to me, Ben?" I whispered, hugging my knees to my chest. "Yeah, I know I should be used to it. Them backing out of stuff, I mean. But no trip has ever meant so much before. This was my dream come true. And now...it's over."

I rested my chin on my knees. "Do you know how that feels, Ben? Did you ever dream about swimming out in the ocean? Just you in miles and miles of blue . . . dancing with seaweed, wiggling in the sand, surfing down waves with the dolphins. And then you woke up and you were *still here*? Still inside four glass walls, with the same dumb old turquoise gravel and an empty treasure chest?"

Ben's mouth made endless imitations of a Cheerio. Maybe fish didn't dream. Maybe they didn't even sleep.

I leaned forward and tapped the glass. Lipman, Bell, the Wright Brothers, and Edison darted over, wiggling like little puppy-fish, ready for a treat. When none came, they made an abrupt about-face, heading toward the fake mermaid in the corner. Ben followed, waving a fin at me.

"That's right, everybody," I said. "Wave good-bye to my fame. My fortune. My *future*. Why? Because of Mom and Dad. Because of them I'm going to stay home this summer. I'm going to a stupid writing class. And the Nice Alarm is going . . . nowhere."

I gazed at the Alarm where it squatted just inches away on my desk. I listened to its soft, precise tick-tick tick-tick tick-tick. I reached out to set the timer, then stopped. What was the use?

I turned away.

That's when I could swear the ticking grew *louder*,

like it was taunting me. Daring me. And instead of tick-tick tick-tick, I heard an insistent do-it do-it.

Before I could change my mind, I set the timer. Five seconds. Then I hit the switch.

Four … three … two …

I held my breath.

Shut my eyes.

Nothing happened.

I sighed and leaned my head on my desk. It didn't matter after all that I couldn't go to the Convention. My invention was a flop. A failure.

Just like me.

Then I felt something tap me gently, *nicely,* on the shoulder. Once. Twice.

The Nice Alarm.

I jerked upright. "It works!" I cried, scooping the Nice Alarm into my hands. I cradled it. Coddled it. All the while dancing around the room, whooping and hollering and then whispering, "It *works!*"

A flood of possibilities rushed over me. TV commercials! Radio campaigns! The Nice Alarm available wherever fine clocks are sold! I could do this. I could. And I had the inklings of a plan for exactly *how* to do it....

I grabbed The List. Snatched up my pencil. Then I scribbled the number eight, and after it:

Find a way to go to the Invention Convention—without them.

SIX

The next morning Hiccup and I rode our bikes to Gadabout Golf, the local miniature golf course. Tucked inside my pack was my mini tool kit. If all went well, I'd be doing more than fishing balls out of the pond for a measly quarter apiece. I had big plans to make big money—part of my even bigger plan to get to the Invention Convention.

But when we skidded our bikes to a stop at the front gate, my big plan turned into a big worry.

Through the paint-chipped fence we saw an extinct volcano. A tilted windmill. A scuttled pirate ship. Moatless castle. Each with ragged paths made of indoor/outdoor carpet that looked older than my grandma, and surrounded by faded AstroTurf in need of a crew cut. Nearby, in the scummy pond, a recording played the burps of long-dead frogs. A neon sign over our heads sputtered the words ADABOUT OLE.

"Oh-oh," my friend said and started to hic.

I wrinkled my nose. The air smelled of warm plastic grass, corn dogs, and rotting lily pads. "It's even worse than last summer," I admitted.

"Are you sure we should go in?" Hiccup asked. "It's likely we'll find mosquitoes in that pond. I fear I could contract malaria."

"I *have* to go in," I answered. "See, I've got it all figured out. I apply here for a job and work every day after summer school. Weekends too. In about a month I'll have enough money to attend the Invention Convention. I'll ride up to San Francisco with Regan, have my meeting with Mr. Patterson, he'll buy the Nice Alarm, and *bingo!* The rest is history."

"Have you discussed this plan with...*her?*"

"Well, no." I chained my bike to a rusty bike-stand. "In fact, Mom thinks we're at Sears, in the plumbing department. I told her if she wouldn't approve my career in sanitation, maybe she'd let me be a garbage disposal repairman." I grinned. "That last part really bugged her."

Hiccup hicked and fiddled with his lock. I could tell he didn't want to look at me. Even though he was bummed about the canceled vacation and our forced enrollment in summer school, he still didn't approve of me needling the love of his life.

"How about Regan?" Hiccup asked, his voice cool. "Have you sought his approval yet?"

"Nope."

My friend hiccupped harder.

"Take it easy, buddy," I said, pulling a thermos of juice from my pack and offering him a drink. "Everything will work out fine. Regan shouldn't mind taking me to the Convention, as long as I pay my own way. And I bet I can get a job here, even if things do look a little..."

"Poverty-stricken?" put in Hiccup. "Abandoned? Destitute? Broke?"

"They can't be *that* broke. See? I'm in luck already." I pointed to a poster hanging lopsided on the front gate. It read Help Wanted.

I smoothed my hair, tucked in my T-shirt, and took some tissue out of my pack to blow my nose. (Gadabout Golf is surrounded by eucalyptus trees, which I'm terminally allergic to.) Hiccup did some nose-work of his own by coating it with white sunscreen. He looked a lot like he'd fallen face first into a container of whipped cream.

I unhooked the Help Wanted poster and tucked it under my arm. "Ready?"

Hiccup sniffed at the air. "One moment." Then he took from his pack a surgical mask. He fit it over his nose and mouth, and tightened the elastic band to hold it in place around the back of his head.

"What's that for?"

"In case of germs."

I sighed. "Well, stay behind me. I don't want the

boss to think that *we* think he's got a disease or something."

We swung open the screechy gate and headed along the path toward the office. It resembled the gingerbread house in *Hansel and Gretel*—complete with concrete candy-cane beams, a stucco sugar-icing roof, and one witch. A live one.

"*Rats!*" I whispered through gritted teeth.

"Where?" Hiccup scanned the path, prancing around on tiptoes.

"It's *her*."

"Her who?"

"That girl. Behind the counter. She worked here last summer. You remember, the one who always eyed us with the Squint of Suspicion."

"Ah (*hic*), yes," said Hiccup. "I am surprised management has yet to fire her. I seem to recall her extreme grouchiness. Perhaps she suffers from anterior metatarsalgia."

"What's that?" I asked, horrified.

Hiccup shrugged. "Sore feet."

"Tug your cap lower," I advised, doing the same. "Maybe she won't recognize us."

I took a deep breath to relax my quaking stomach. There was something about the girl's squint that always made me feel uneasy. Guilty. Like I'd just robbed a bank, and she *knew*.

As we got closer, I noticed she'd grown taller than

me since last year. That was the only change. Her hair was still the color of rice. On one side of her face it swooped down, curling like a C beneath her chin. On the other side she tucked it behind her ear, showing off a golf-ball earring. Pinned to her Gadabout Golf T-shirt was a tag that read in cheery letters: Hi! My Name Is Hayley Barker! But her expression wasn't cheery. Her eyes glowed with such a cold blue, they gave me an ice-cream headache.

I strode up to the counter and cleared my throat.

"Yes?" she said, the word a challenge. She leaned one elbow against the counter and gave me the dreaded Squint of Suspicion. Then she noticed Hic. "What is this, a stickup?"

I squelched that just-robbed-a-bank feeling and opened my mouth to answer.

Then my nose started to tickle.

And tingle.

And itch.

Without another warning, I let loose the mother of all sneezes. Plus the father. And the six children.

"*Yes?*" she demanded again.

By that time I was too busy snuffling and snorking to speak. Instead, I held up the Help Wanted sign.

"Yes, I can see you need help," she said. "There's a pay phone around back if you want to call 9-1-1."

I coughed and blew my nose. "You don't under-stand," I gurgled. "I'm here to apply for the job."

"Not so loud!" she said in a fierce whisper. She glanced over her shoulder. "There's no job, okay? So just hightail it out of here. Now." She turned her back on me to organize the already-organized golf clubs and scorecards.

"Let's go," Hiccup said, tugging my arm.

I ignored him.

"Excuse me," I said in a firm voice, "but I want to apply for this job. May I please speak to someone in charge?"

"*I'm* in charge," Hayley announced in her whisper.

"How can you be?" I challenged. "You're just a kid!"

"I'll be a *seventh* grader," she shot back, "and if I say there's no job, *there's no job!* Why don't you try Golf 'n' Goodies, down at the lake? I'll bet they've got plenty of money to hire summer help. Huh. They think they're so great with their glitzy video arcade and skateboard park and batting cages and bumper cars. And fifty-dollar cash prizes for holes in one!"

Hiccup and I exchanged glances. "But–" I began.

"No *but*'s!" She shook her head, the golf-ball earrings swinging. "We don't need any help here, thank you very much. We're getting along just fine. Even with hoodlums like you jumping the fence after hours, trashing the Castle moat, or dumping soap flakes in the Volcano."

"Pardon me, miss," Hiccup interrupted, "but

Sneeze here is not a hoodlum. He's an inventor. He doesn't destroy ... he *creates*."

Hayley rolled her eyes. "I suppose you want a job too?"

"Why, yes. Something indoors, perhaps. The smell of AstroTurf gives me cephalalgia."

"What's that?"

"Headache," I answered for him. Some of Hiccup's medical knowledge was rubbing off on me. "Anyway," I went on, "Golf 'n' Goodies is too far to bike. And they're not hiring. You are."

"No, we're not," she argued.

"Hayley!" a voice called.

Her eyes widened. "You'd better leave." She shooed us away like we were pesky flys. "That's the boss, and he doesn't like your kind."

"I thought *you* were in charge," I said.

"Hayley!" called the same voice. "Where are the Band-Aids? The cash register attacked me again. Can't seem to figure out what's wrong with the thingamajig that's supposed to make the doohickey open and close automatically."

The voice became a man who'd entered the office through a side door, his arm outstretched, thumb up. The thumb was swollen and bleeding.

"Daddy, are you okay?" Hayley cried. She rushed to examine his hand.

"I'm fine. Not to worry. Oh ... hello," he said, noticing us. He nodded, waved, then winced. "Are these friends of yours, Hayley?"

She snorted. Ignoring us, she took a first-aid kit from under the counter and began to swab at her dad's thumb with alcohol-smelling stuff that Hiccup probably knew the Latin name for.

"You should have that thumb X-rayed," Hiccup advised. "You could have a fracture of the metacarpal bone, which would greatly restrict your flexion and extension movements."

"Are you a doctor?" Mr. Barker teased.

"No," I answered, elbowing Hiccup in the ribs. "We're mechanics." I pulled the mini tool kit from my pack and presented it with a bow. "Have tools, will travel. I bet I could fix that cash register of yours in a snap."

"Could you, now?" Mr. Barker said.

"Absolutely. I could untilt that windmill too. And get the moat flowing again. Even find the missing *G*'s in your neon sign."

"Hmmm." Mr. Barker peered at the Band-Aid his daughter had just wound around his thumb, then thumbed her gently on the nose with it. "Thanks, honey. You're a peach."

She flashed him a shy smile.

He ruffled her hair, then turned to me. "Grab your gear and follow me. Let's put you to the test right now."

I trotted after him into a cluttered back office, Hayley and Hiccup at my heels. The register was an old, pre-electronic style. It teetered atop a tower of overflowing files, its cash drawer gaping like an oversized mouth.

"It appears to have gastritis," Hiccup observed.

"What's that?" Hayley asked.

"Upset stomach."

I ignored them and set to work. Tinker here. Tinker there. A little oil. Press a button, and ...

"Ta-da!" With a gleeful *ching!* the drawer slid in and out with ease.

"Well, I'll be doggone," Mr. Barker said as I repacked my tools. "Hayley, put these two boys on the payroll. I think I've finally found my hired help."

Hayley shot me an iceberg-like glance. It melted when she spoke to her dad. "But we can't afford to hire anyone right now." She hauled out a financial ledger. "Look at these figures! Look at these bills! And if we don't start pulling in more golfers, we'll have to close by summer's end."

"Now, now," he soothed.

"Daddy, this is *serious*. Besides, you don't need these . . . these *mechanics*, when you've got me. I could've tightened those screws myself! And there's a lot more I can do around here—"

"Hayley, you do too much already," Mr. Barker said. "I want you to have a little fun this summer for a change. Now, boys, can you work afternoons? One to five? Great. My daughter will get you a couple of Gadabout T-shirts, and fill you in on the details. When you're finished, meet me at the Castle. Having a little trouble with the drawbridge. That's hole number fifteen. Take a left at the tombstones and a right at the Swiss cheese. Can't miss it."

"Yessir!" I saluted. "By the way, if you like my work, do you think I could have a small advance against my wages? I owe a little money and—"

"Sure, sure," Mr. Barker said, digging out his wallet. "You can have the advance now. How much do you need?"

I couldn't believe my luck! I'd be able to pay off Regan for the Nice Alarm by Monday after all. "Just six dollars and eighty cents, sir."

"*Daddy,*" Hayley pleaded, her voice desperate.

"Now, sweetheart, I remember when I was a boy and what it was like to need a few extra bucks." He peeled off several bills, pushed them into my hand, then hurried off.

"Seems you're not really in charge after all," I said to Hayley.

She didn't look at me. "Maybe I am and maybe I'm not. You'll find out soon enough."

She started slapping stuff on the counter. "Here are your T-shirts, restroom keys, and time cards. You can only work a few hours a week 'cause you're under age. We'll plan out an official schedule later. You get minimum wage. Period. And don't dare hit my dad up for any more advances. Or raises. Employees have been taking advantage of his niceness the last two years, and he lets them get away with it. Well, I'm not going to. Not anymore."

"Yeah, but I didn't mean to—"

"I don't want to hear it," Hayley cut me off. "Just make sure you two behave yourselves. That means no showing up late for work. No freebies for your hoodlum friends. No after-hour swimming parties in the moat. Don't think you can get away with *anything*, because you can't."

She turned those cold blue eyes on me full force. My head felt as if I'd just eaten a triple-scoop ice-cream cone—in one bite.

"Because," she added, "I'll be watching you...."

SEVEN

"No, no, no, no, *no*," Regan said later that afternoon. Hiccup and I had stopped by the Tool Box on the way home from Gadabout Golf. "No, I am *not* taking you to the Convention with me. No way, no how, no thank you."

"If it's the money you're worried about," I said, "I'm good for it. Look, here's the six-eighty I owe you." I laid out the bills plus change in a neat little row on the counter.

Quick as a magician, Regan made the money disappear into the cash register.

"And there's plenty more where that came from," I continued. "We got *jobs*."

"Lifetime enslavement better describes it," Hiccup put in.

I agreed. Mr. Barker had given us a mile-long list of things he needed repaired, painted, patched, spruced, and adjusted. It would take us till the end of summer to finish—next summer, that is. Hiccup and I spent most of our first day at hole number eighteen trying to fix the leaky Pirate Ship. We were "at sea" so long, Hic swore he'd contracted scurvy.

"It's not just the money," Regan was saying. "I don't want to baby-sit for four days. I've got things to do. Places to go. People to meet."

"So do I." I pulled Mr. Patterson's letter from my pack. "No one except Hiccup has seen this. But I trust you, and I think you have a right to know."

Regan eyed the letter as if it was a rattlesnake ready to strike. "Who's it from, my ex-wife?"

"Which one?" I asked.

"Ha-ha." He wiped his greasy hands down the front of his T-shirt (which read Screwdrivers-R-Us), then snatched the letter from me.

As he read, I shifted from one foot to the other. Bit my nails. Tapped my cheek.

C'mon, Regan, I thought, willing him to agree. You've got to take me along. You've got to....

I glanced at Hiccup. He crossed his fingers and began a series of skittery sympathy hics.

At last Regan refolded the letter and handed it back. He didn't look at me. Didn't speak to me. After about ten years he said, his voice soft, "Okay, kiddo. I'll have to check with your old man and lady. But if they say it's okay, then I'll take you along."

I realized I'd been holding my breath. I let it out slow. "Thanks, Regan. Thanks a whole lot." I held out my hand. It disappeared within his massive, rough fingers.

"Well, I couldn't have anyone sayin' I stood in the way of genius." He cleared his throat. "But I got rules, you know. No whining. No homesickness. No back-seat driving. Also, you'd better stick by my side at all times. I don't want you getting lost or kidnapped. You listening to me, kiddo?"

"No," I admitted, grinning. I was already picturing the headlines: *Nice Kid Makes Nice Bundle with Nice Alarm. Whiz Kid Wakes up World—Nicely. Boy Wonder Rings in Success with 'Alarming' Invention.*

Of course, all the kids at school would read the papers. As I sauntered throughout the junior high, they'd point and whisper in awe: *"That's him! He invented the Nice Alarm!"* Guys would ask for my autograph. Girls would giggle and swoon. Even Hayley Barker's ice-cream eyes would melt at my approach. And I'd never, ever, *ever* be picked last again for a P. E. softball team.

"Plus, we'll split all expenses," Regan was saying. "Gas, food, hotel, Convention fees. I figure it'll cost us five hundred bucks apiece. I'll need half of your half by next Saturday for a deposit. That's two hundred and fifty dollars. Not pesos. Not drachmas. Not lire. Not M&M's. *American* dollars. Got it?"

"I know what dollars are, Regan."

"Uh-huh." He grabbed the pencil from behind his ear. "What's your phone number? I'll give your old man a call."

"Um, he's been kinda busy lately," I said, "working at three schools and stuff. I'll have him call you in a couple of weeks."

Regan grunted, which I translated to mean yes. Actually, if I could swing it, I didn't plan to tell Mom and Dad about the trip until the last minute, when it was too late to say no. I had a sneaking suspicion they wouldn't want me traveling five hundred miles with a guy who had a hydraulic compressor called "Mother" tattooed across his chest.

I started to thank Regan again. "If there's anything else I can do, just name it."

He waved us away. "Yeah, yeah. Now beat it. Closing time."

Hic and I slapped a high five. His hiccups seemed to chirp with joy.

We rushed to the door. When I turned the knob, I felt like a whole new world was opening up for me. A world where so much could happen. A world where *I* could make so much happen....

But minutes later, *whump!* The door to that world slammed shut.

"Um, I know now is not the best time to mention this," Hiccup said as we pedaled home. "But just how do you plan to acquire two hundred and fifty dollars in one week?"

"Working at Gadabout, of course," I answered. "I figure if I slave away every hour the law says I can, plus earn a few extra bucks scooping golf balls out of that scummy pond, by next Saturday I should have earned about—"

"Fifty dollars," Hiccup said.

I screeched to a halt. "That can't be right," I argued, pulling a notepad from my pack. I scribbled some figures. Bit the end of my pencil. Totaled the numbers.

"Rats! It *is* right. Unless I sell a kidney or something, I'm gonna be two hundred dollars short!"

"Actually, four hundred and fifty dollars short," Hiccup said. "Have you forgotten the first two-fifty is just a deposit?"

"I know, I know." I slumped over my handlebars. "And Regan will probably want all of it before we leave. The Convention's only a month away. How can I earn enough money in time?"

Hiccup shook his head. "The probability of your success is extremely low. Now I understand why your parents were forced to cancel our vacation."

I glared at him.

"Not that I'm letting them off the hook," he added hastily.

I shoved the pencil and notepad into my pack, and slung it over my shoulders.

"You may have all my earnings," Hiccup said, "and pay me back when you can."

I looked him straight in the eye, so he'd know how much his offer meant to me. "Thanks, Hic. But I can't let you do that."

"But I *want* to."

"No way. You never have enough money for drawing paper and ink and stuff."

"That's true." He fell silent for a moment. "But if you won't take my money, what *will* you do?"

"I don't know." With a sigh I pushed off toward home. "I really don't know."

EIGHT

*T*hings to Do to Bug Mom and Dad

9. *Don't get up on time.*
10. *Use all the hot water in the shower.*
11. *Don't flush.*
12. *?*

"Steve!" Mom called from downstairs on Monday morning. "Better get a move on, or you'll miss the bus to summer school!"

"Okay!" I hurried into my clothes. Then I thought, Wait a minute. What is this "Mister Nice Guy" stuff? It's not like I *want* to go to summer school. . . .

With a smile I took out The List and wrote next to number twelve:

Miss the bus so they have to drive me.

After that I changed my clothes. Twice.
Said a personal good-bye to each of my fish. Twice.
Then cleaned my room. (Once was enough.)

I met Dad on the stairs, heading down to the kitchen. He was finger-rumpling his wet hair. "Hey, what's with the long shower this morning?" he complained with a shiver. "You didn't leave me any hot water."

"I was dirty," I said.

"Well, next time have a little consideration for other showerers in the family. Pneumonia might be Hiccup's idea of a fun way to start the day, but it's not mine." He hurried to pour himself a cup of hot coffee.

I slid into my seat and blew my nose. Loudly.

"Steve, *please*," Mom said, closing her eyes as if in pain. "That's disgusting. How many times have I asked you not to do that at the table?"

"Seven hundred forty-two," I answered, "and a half."

"Eat," she ordered, sliding a plate and glass in front of me.

I stared at the eggs, bacon, hash browns, toast, and juice. "I'm not hungry."

"But you asked me to fix you a big breakfast!"

"Yeah, well, now I'm not hungry."

Mom made her cow-giving-birth noise. I'd have to add a number thirteen to The List:

Look at my plate, then say I'm not hungry.

"I'll eat it," Dad volunteered. He shuffled aside a pile of papers he'd been correcting to make room for my plate. "Do we have any salsa?"

"At least eat the toast, Steve," Mom said, tugging on her lab coat, "and do it fast. I don't know what's gotten into you this morning, but if you don't stop dawdling you'll miss the—" she glanced out the window—"the bus! There goes the bus! Now I'll have to drive you to school!" The next noise she made sounded like a cow giving birth to a tractor.

I hummed.

Mom threw Dad a hopeful glance. "Unless *you* can drop him off...."

"No can do." He splunked ketchup onto his bacon and, accidentally, his tie. "I'm teaching in Riverside today. Opposite direction. And I'm already late."

Mom stomped around, grabbing her purse and keys and the petri dish from the fridge.

"Somebody's not in a very good mood this morning," Dad murmured.

"That's because *somebody* left the front door open when *somebody* went out to get the newspaper," Mom answered, "and the neighbor's dog got in and tracked mud all over the kitchen floor that *somebody else* had just mopped!"

Hmmm, not a bad idea—even if it wasn't mine. I mentally added *Leave the door open every time you go in and out of the house* to The List, noticing Dad had grown *very* quiet.

Hiccup met me on the front steps of the school a few minutes before nine.

"I assumed you missed the bus," he said, peering over my shoulder to catch a glimpse of Mom. He waved, but she'd peeled out of the parking lot, gravel spraying. His smile faded. "*She* must've have been most irritated."

"Yeah, ain't it great?" I said. "C'mon, let's get this over with."

We tromped down the hall. I noticed he limped a bit, but I didn't ask what was wrong. I've learned never to ask Hiccup how he is, because he'll *always* tell me. "I think we're in Room Seven," I said instead. "Lucky seven."

"Surely you jest," Hiccup commented. "Look who's lounging outside the door."

Goldie.

"Oh, man, she's the *last* person I want to see right now," I said. "Can you believe she came all the way over here just to gloat? Well, I'm not going to take this lying down."

I marched up to her, arms open in surrender. "Okay, Goldie, I bow to your superior spying powers. You are the Master of Nosiness. The Queen of Snoop."

She blinked. "Say what?"

"You were right," I said. "I'm not going on vacation. I'm not going to the Invention Convention. I'm stuck right here in summer school. So gloat if you want. I'll give you sixty whole seconds, but that's it. Then I want you to go home—to your great summer vacation."

I stood ready for that smug I-told-you-so smile. But instead Goldie said, "I'm not here to gloat. I'm going to summer school too."

"What?!" Hiccup and I chorused together.

She heaved a sigh overflowing with misery. "My mother, the Vice-Principal, was promoted to Principal. So now we're not going to Hollywood."

"I'm sorry," I said, as much for Goldie as myself. I mean, now I'd have to spend another month putting up with her spying and prying and listening to hourly bulletins that her mother was the new you-know-what.

I just hoped she'd forgotten that I owed her . . . *information*.

"Hiccup," she said, "did I notice you limping?"

His face brightened. "Why, yes. Sneeze and I have secured jobs at Gadabout Golf. The work entails a great deal of outdoor activity, and I believe I'm suffering from a heel spur."

"Is that a cowboy disease?" she asked.

"No, it's a—"

The first bell rang.

"We'd better go in," I said, and yanked the door open.

There sat Pierre. And Ace.

And Hayley.

What were *they* doing here?

"Zair—zat's 'im!" Pierre cried out, pointing at me. Several kids I'd never seen before turned to stare. "'E eez zee one I tell you about. Zee one zat make zee alarm clock bomb!"

"It's *not* a bomb—" I said.

"It looked like a bomb," yawned Ace.

"It detonated on Hiccup's nose," Goldie explained to the class.

"I thought the accident might have caused a septal hematoma," Hiccup put in. "But I never even suffered an epistaxis."

Goldie asked, "Is that a cab disease?"

"No, it's a nosebleed that—"

"This is all your fault," Hayley interrupted. She squinted at me. "The first time I set eyes on you, I knew you were up to no good."

"What's my fault?" I said. "What did I do?"

"As if you didn't know ..."

"Did 'e try out one of zee inventions on you?" Pierre asked with sympathy. "And eet was—how you say—a lemon, was eet not?" He shook his head. "A pity for someone so sweet to suffer somezing so sour..."

Everyone laughed. Not with me. *At* me. As always.

I couldn't stand another four weeks of this. I just couldn't.

"Uh—I think I have to use the boys' room," I said, backing toward the door. "In Kentucky."

I turned to flee.

And plowed right into somebody's stomach.

I looked up.

He looked down.

Scribbler.

NINE

is-ter Wy-att!" Scribbler said with a phony
smile. His hand clomped onto my shoulder. "What a
pleasure to see you."

Translation: *Caught ya!*

I wiggled a bit under his grip, feeling like a hooked
fish. "Uh, the pleasure is mine."

"Not at all. I'm delighted we'll be working together
again." He gave my shoulder a squeeze. "And delighted we can now have that little chat we were supposed to have on Friday. Mr. Wyatt, a moment of your
time?"

He steered me toward the hall. I prepared to be
dropped into a pit of snapping crocodiles. Or alliga-
tors. Or both.

"I'll keep this quick and painless," Scribbler said.
"Raise your right hand and repeat after me: 'I promise
never to bring an invention to summer school.'"

"I promise," I said weakly, "never to bring an invention to summer school."

"'Even,'" Scribbler went on, "'if I think it's the most

healthful, helpful labor-saving device ever to be created on this earth.'"

"Uh, yeah," I agreed. "What you said."

"'I promise to do this for the welfare of my fellow students…'"

He must've been thinking of the day my Electric Chalkboard Squeegee blew a fuse, decapitating an innocent bystander: the world globe.

"'and the thread-hanging sanity of my teacher…'"

No, he was remembering the time my Multi-Pencil Turbo Sharpener fired a dozen number twos into the air, pulverizing a fluorescent light.

"'or else.'"

"Or else," I said with a gulp. I didn't want to ask what he meant. Funny how two little words can conjure up so many pictures of death, disease, and destruction.

Scribbler's face loomed to my eye level. "I'm serious about this, Mr. Wyatt," he said with that familiar frown in his voice. "Do we understand each other?"

I bobbed my head.

"Good." He opened the classroom door. "Allow me to escort you to your seat."

With his hand still buddy-buddy-like on my shoulder, he steered me to a desk beside Hiccup, in front of Goldie, and directly behind Hayley.

She turned to squint at me. "What are you," she demanded, "the teacher's pet?"

"Not exactly," I mumbled.

I slumped into my chair. Who could've known I'd get stuck with Scribbler as my teacher? *Again?*

Mom and Dad, that's who. They'd signed me up for the class, so they must've known. They just didn't have the guts to tell me I was doomed. Doomed to spend another four miserable weeks with Scribbler-the-Mighty-Invention-Hater.

I took out The List and scrawled a few more choice items:

15. Make them come to school to drop off the homework I "forgot."
16. Ask them for help with my homework, then let them do it while I watch TV.
17. Tell them Hiccup's dogs ate my homework.

The last bell rang. As kids scrambled to take their seats, Scribbler slipped over to his desk, eased his special notepad and pen into the third drawer, then strode to the front of the room.

"Good morning, people," he said, "and welcome to 'Recipe for a Book.' For those of you who don't know me, my name is Mr. Powell. I will be your master chef. Together we will chop, slice, dice, measure, and mix the ingredients necessary to bake a delicious book."

He paused as if he'd said something clever and was

waiting for us to applaud. When no one did, he cleared his throat and continued.

"Today we'll concentrate on ideas for your books. How to come up with them, which ones are the best to write about—and why. Most important, I'll show you how to turn your ideas into books other people will want to read. But first, let's take roll."

Scribbler opened his attendance book and started down the list of names.

"Hayley Barker, Luisa Contreras, Hector Denardo…

"Mr. Denardo, you look very healthy today," Scribbler commented. "Do I see a hint of sunburn on your face?"

"Actually," Hiccup answered, "I believe it's a case of roseola."

"Is that a flower disease?" Goldie asked.

"No, it's a —"

Scribbler held up a hand for silence and finished attendance. "Trudy Laux, Peter Noel, Sherry Shahan, Ace, Daniel Tanaka…

"Ace, I'm surprised to see you here," he exclaimed. "I thought you'd planned to hang out this summer."

Ace lazily stretched his legs into the aisle and drawled, "I am."

"*Ah-ha!*" Goldie whispered. She poked me with her pencil.

"Ouch," I grumbled. "Quit it."

She poked twice more.

"What are you trying to do," I whispered, "give me lead poisoning?"

"We *have* to talk," Goldie murmured with excitement. She swiped at her hair and leaned forward. "It's about Ace. And the ... *information* you owe me."

"Later," I grunted. "Like, maybe, Christmas."

"Recess," Goldie insisted. "And I want to talk to you about Gadabout Golf. I'm thinking of having my birthday party there in August."

"Uh, I'll probably be busy."

"I wasn't going to *invite* you." Goldie made a face. "That's all I need, to have you sneezing on my cake. No, I want you to get me some free passes for my guests."

Hayley must've overheard our whispers, because she turned toward me ver-ry slow-ly. Her usual Squint of Suspicion had transformed into a Squint of Death.

I coughed. "Sorry, Goldie. Can't help you."

Both girls glared at me so fiercely, my head felt like a marshmallow on a stick over a campfire. I pretended to concentrate on what Scribbler was saying.

"So where do authors get their ideas?" He tapped his temple. "From up here. Write about people, situations, or things that are important to you. Important to your life."

Scribbler chalked the last four words on the board and underlined them.

"If you pick a topic you enjoy writing about, that will come through in your work—and your audience will probably enjoy reading about it too."

Pierre raised his hand. "But what eef you do not like to write? I want to bake desserts, not books. To me, writing eez not light and flaky, like zee pastry. Eet eez heavy and tasteless, like zee Pop-Tart."

Scribbler glanced at his desk. His lips twitched and he sighed.

"As I tried to explain," the teacher said, "the trick is to think of a topic that is *very* important to you. The more you enjoy your topic, the more you'll enjoy writing about it. It won't be a chore, but a pleasure."

Pierre rolled his eyes.

Scribbler didn't notice. He clapped his hands and said, "Okay, people, brainstorming time. I want you to form groups of five. You're to discuss with your group things you like to do, or places you've enjoyed visiting, or important people in your lives. Then jot down the topics you think you'd like to write about. I'll check on you in a few minutes."

He hurried to his desk, took out his special notepad and pen, and started scribbling. I suspect he volunteered to teach this class so he could write his book with us—and get paid for it!

The rest of us grumbled. But we scraped and

scuffed our desks across the floor, forming little sing-around-the-campfire circles, as if we were at summer camp.

Except this camp was no picnic. My group featured Goldie, Ace, Pierre, and the ever-squinting Hayley.

"Since my mother is the Principal," Goldie announced, "I think she'd want me assigned as your group leader. It's the least she can do, after she ruined my summer vacation."

"I know zee feeling!" Pierre complained. He twisted his beret in his hands. "Zis eez an outrage! I am fur-ee-ous wis Mama. She say to me, Zee cooking class eez too expensive. We need zee inexpensive, practical class, like zee writing. Ah! Such a waste of my talent! Would she want zee Julia Child to be practical and, how you say, cheep?"

"Don't put all the blame on your mom," Hayley groused. She folded her arms and squinted at me. "Maybe she was swayed by a *bad influence*."

Her gaze made my nose itch. I sneezed and said, "What are you saying, that it's *my* fault you're in this stupid class?"

"Absolutely. If you and your hoodlum friend hadn't come begging for a job and blabbing about summer school, my dad never would've found out about this class and signed me up."

"Hold on here—"

Hayley cut me off. "'You spend too much time at the golf course,' Daddy said. 'You need to get out and have fun with people your own age.'" She shoved her hair behind one ear and set the golf-ball earrings swaying. "Huh. Some fun I'll have if while I'm gone he..." she stopped. Stared out the window.

But not before I caught a glimpse of her eyes. They sort of glistened, like they do right before you cry.

"Oh, never mind." Haley's voice sounded hoarse. "You wouldn't understand."

No one said anything for a long minute. Ace raised an eyebrow.

"Well," Pierre said, breaking the silence, "I for one vow nevare to speek wis Mama again. Or better yet—I repeat everytheeng she say! Ha-ha! That drive her, how you say, crazee!"

"That's a good one," I chuckled, and took out The List. Just as I jotted down number eighteen, Goldie snatched The List from my hands.

"What's this," she asked, "your *diary*? Ooh, let me read all the dirt!"

"The only entry you'll see," Ace said with a yawn, "is *Today, blew my nose into one hundred sixty-four tissues—and one sock.*"

"Very funny," I said. "Now give it back."

Goldie nudged Pierre in the ribs. "This *is* funny. Looks effective too. Take a peek."

He read over her shoulder. "'Theengs to Do to Bug Mom and Dad.' *Oui*. I *like* eet," he said. "May I copy a few ideas? I like to try zees one and zat one tonight."

Goldie laughed. "Yeah, me too. These are great, Sneeze!"

"Well, sure," I said. "Go ahead. Help yourselves." I felt a warm glow in my stomach.

"Zank you. You are most kind." Pierre patted me on the back. "Do you 'ave more ways zan zis?"

"Oh, sure—at home," I lied. I couldn't help myself. In all the years I'd known them, Pierre and Goldie had *never* acted so nice to me. Besides, I *could* have more ways at home. All I had to do was invent them.

"'Ow many more?"

"Um…" I bit my lip. "Fifty or so."

"Ahhh," Pierre said. "I would pay beeg money for a leest like that."

"You *would*?"

A hand clomped onto my shoulder. Scribbler's hand. "So, how we doing here?"

"Um, okay, I guess," I said.

"Not okay at *all*," Goldie argued. "It's hard to come up with good ideas for a story."

Scribbler pulled a chair over and sat next to me. "Keep in mind," he said, "your books don't have to be *stories*. They can be nonfiction too. A biography, a how-to book, whatever."

"It's still hard to come up with an idea," Goldie insisted.

"Not if you concentrate on things you enjoy. For example, Miss Laux, what do you like doing more than *anything*?"

Goldie grinned. "Snooping."

"Okay, so you could write a biography of a famous spy. Or a gossip columnist."

"Hmmmm," she said, the word dripping with plots to be hatched.

Scribbler turned to Pierre. "How about you, Mr. Noel? What do you like doing best?"

Pierre touched his chest. "Moi? I *bake*."

"So write about baking."

Pierre gasped. "Zat's eet! A cookbook! I could write zee most dee-leee-cious cookbook in zee world!"

Scribbler nodded. "Excellent. Now you, Mr. Wyatt. We've all experienced your love of inventions. Any ideas of how to write about them?"

"Well," I began, "I suppose I could write a history of American inventors. Maybe a biography of Thomas Edison or something."

"That's fine," Scribbler said. "Of course, there are already dozens of biographies out there. And dozens of cookbooks. The key to writing good nonfiction is to choose a fresh angle on your topic that's never been tried before. In other words, find a hole, and fill it. Find a need, and satisfy it."

A faint alarm rang inside my head.

Find a need, and satisfy it. . . .

The ringing grew louder.

Write what's important to you, important to your life. . . .

The ringing changed to a great chiming of bells, pealing with the sound of ideas. Brilliant ideas.

The recess bell clanged.

"Class dismissed," Scribbler said.

I felt Goldie poke me. "Sneeze, about that *information . . .*"

I shook my head. Leaped up. Grabbed Hiccup by the arm. "Quick!" I said. "Goldie's after me. Let's go!"

We streaked out of the room, me dragging my friend down the hall.

"Where are we going?" he asked.

"Boys' room. Got something to tell you. *Hurry.*"

I threw open the bathroom door. Peeked under the stalls. Whirled to face Hiccup. "Good—we're alone."

"Would you kindly tell me what we're doing in here?" he said, pinching his lips with distaste. "You know how I dislike using school restrooms. They harbor a multitude of bacteria that current disinfectants can't—"

"You don't have to touch anything. You don't even have to breathe. Just stand there and *listen*." I gave his shoulders a little shake. "Hiccup, it came to me in a flash, when Scribbler was talking about our book projects. I'm going to write a book. A great book. A book that every kid in our class—no, every kid in our *school*—is going to want to read!"

I did a little jig across the tiled floor. "And not only will they want to read this book, they're going to want to *buy* it. They'll pay big money. Big!"

My friend just stood there, eyes wide with confusion.

"Don't you understand what this means?" I asked. "I'm going to the Convention. I'm *going!*"

Hiccup began to hic with excitement. "Yes, I see now," he said. "But—but how will you publish this book?"

I nibbled a fingernail. "I can type it in the school's computer lab, no problem. I wonder if I could use the office photocopier to make copies? I bet I'll need at least a hundred. Maybe two hundred. Three."

"I advise caution," Hiccup said. "How can you be so sure that your book will reach best-seller status?"

"Because," I said with a smile, "it's called *101 Ways to Bug Your Parents*."

T E N

When school ended at noon, Hiccup and I scampered out of the building to catch the bus before Goldie could catch *us*. I felt like a mouse being stalked by a hungry cat. But maybe if I scurried around long enough, she'd grow tired of the chase and pounce on some other kid for her mysterious *information*.

The bus was late.

"Sneeze—wait up!"

I turned to see Goldie charging down the front steps, her hair rippling behind her in the wind like a battle flag.

Rats. Cornered again!

Just then, a battered car sputtered up to the curb. "Why, if it isn't my hired help!" a familiar voice called through an open window. "Need a lift, boys?"

"Sure, Mr. Barker!" Hiccup and I plunged into the backseat. "Uh, could you step on it, please?"

He laughed. "Don't want to be late for work, huh? I'm just waiting for Hayley. Here she comes."

"Daddy," she scolded, flinging open the front door. "I thought we agreed I'd take the bus. Who's looking

after Gadabout? We can't afford to shut down every day at noon just so you can pick me up and—"

She froze. Squinted. "What are *you* two doing here?" she demanded.

"I offered them a lift," Mr. Barker said. "And that's no way to talk to our employees. Or our friends."

Hayley snorted, but got into the car and slammed the door. She hugged her notebook to her chest and didn't say a word, but I could practically hear the wheels turning in her head. Probably calculating the gas mileage from school to Gadabout so she could deduct it from our paychecks.

The car rattled away into traffic just as Goldie reached the curb. She coughed in a cyclone of exhaust. I smiled and waved to her out the back window.

"So, how was writing class?" Mr. Barker asked cheerfully. "What did you do today?"

"We brainstormed topics we wish to write about," Hiccup explained. "Tomorrow Mr. Powell will have topic conferences with each of us to approve our choices. I believe I'm going to write an in-depth history of comic books in America, which began, you know, with *Action Comics* in 1938."

I looked at my friend with shock. I'd thought for sure he'd choose a health-related subject for his book. Something like *Diseases I Have Visited* or *Cough Syrup Is Our Friend*.

"Sneeze here," Hiccup went on, "is writing a book which should prove instructive, humorous, and quite lucrative. It's called—"

I elbowed him quickly in the ribs. "Uh, I haven't decided on the final title yet, *have I*, Hiccup?"

"Ouch! I mean (*hic*), no."

Call it Kids' Intuition, but I strongly suspected parents wouldn't appreciate the subject matter of my book. At least not until I'd published a sequel to even things out: *101 Ways to Bug Your Children.*

"Hayley, what about you?" Mr. Barker was asking. "What's your book about?"

"Daddy, I don't think I should get too wrapped up in this class," she answered. "I mean, what if you find out you really need me at Gadabout? Who's going to greet customers and take money and check in golf clubs while I'm at school and you're busy fixing the drawbridge? You can't do everything."

"Now, now," her father soothed. "You worry too much. That's supposed to be *my* job. You're young! You should be out having fun with your friends, not spending every moment at some run-down putt-putt golf course."

"I *love* Gadabout," insisted Hayley, her voice fierce.

"I know, I know. But there's got to be life after golf." Mr. Barker chuckled, then glanced at us in his rearview mirror. "Besides, I have plenty of help in the afternoons, thanks to our new expert mechanics."

Hayley snorted again, but didn't argue. Still, taking no chances, Hiccup and I stayed out of her way once we reached Gadabout. We ate our sack lunches near hole number nine, the Windmill, which is the farthest from the office.

I licked peanut butter off my fingers, then plucked several sheets of toilet paper from my jeans pocket. "Here are the notes I made while hiding out in the bathroom during recess. I've got it all worked out. If I charge five dollars a book, I'll need to sell fifty copies. That will earn me the two hundred and fifty dollars I owe Regan for the Convention deposit."

My friend gave a worrisome hic. "Your sales projections might be too high, Sneeze. That's a great quantity of books."

"Not really," I said. "I'll bet every kid in our class will want one, and every kid in Ms. McLoughlin's class next door. That's fifty sales right there. And once word gets out, the third and fourth graders will be down on their knees *begging* for copies too. That's another two hundred and fifty dollars, and my debt is cleared. Easy as snap, crackle, pop!"

Hiccup studied my notes. "'Ten-page book,'" he read, "'with ten bugging suggestions on first nine pages, eleven on the last. Stapled together.'" He double-hicked. "I believe five dollars is a mite expensive for something so slipshod."

"Slipshod! Don't you know the old saying 'You

can't judge a book by its cover?' Well, nobody's gonna care what this book *looks* like. It's the ideas *inside* that are important. And I'm selling those for only five cents a suggestion—with the 101st one thrown in for free! That's a bargain."

"I suppose," Hiccup said. "But what about your supplies? Paper, staples. How will you pay for those?"

I munched on an apple. "I'll have to keep working here, I guess." That prospect didn't bother me. Sure, at times I felt buried when I saw how much stuff Mr. Barker wanted us to do. Some of the machinery looked old and tricky. Hopeless. But figuring out ways to fix it all would be a fun challenge, make me a better inventor, *and* bring me closer to my dream....

Big Ben at hole number four chimed one o'clock. I crumpled my lunch sack and threw it in the trash. "Time to start work. Mr. Barker wants us to fix the Volcano today. He says it's burping, not rumbling. Probably gobbled too many golf balls." I bent to pick up my toolbox.

Voices drifted in the warm breeze.

I cocked my head. "Did you hear that?"

"Hear what?" Hiccup asked.

"It sounded like . . ." I shivered. The cold worm-slithers had returned.

Goldie.

"I'd like to rent the golf course for the whole evening," she was saying in her best my-mother-is-the-Principal tone. "It's for my birthday, you know. A costume party. Everyone will be dressed like famous Hollywood movie stars. I'm coming as Marilyn Monroe. I always wanted to see my name in lights."

The voices grew closer. Coming this way.

"I'm in charge of all the bookings." Hayley. Sounding boss-ish. "So I can make your reservation now, if you want."

"I told you, I want to talk to your boss first. I want his promise that everything will be ready in time."

"My father is very busy now," Hayley said. "But *I* can promise you that—"

The voices. Coming 'round the bend.

"Maybe I should have my party at Golf 'n' Goodies," Goldie threatened.

"No, no, my father will be happy to talk to you. I think he's working on the Windmill today. That's right down this path—"

"Quick!" I whispered to Hiccup. "Run!"

We looked around. Bumped into each other. No place to hide. No time to get there...

"In here!" I pushed Hiccup through the tiny window of the Windmill. "And whatever you do, don't get the hiccups!"

I wriggled in behind him. We crouched down on

the gritty floor, blinking in the half-dark. The place smelled like cat pee, year-old hot dogs, and dust.

"Daddy?" Hayley called. "Daddy, there's someone here to see you...."

Footsteps encircled the Windmill.

"There's his toolbox," Goldie said. "He must be around somewhere."

"That's not his box. It belongs to our mechanic."

"You mean *Sneeze*?" Goldie snickered. "That's a joke."

"He happens to be a very good mechanic," Hayley replied, her tone cool.

Goldie whooped. "Oh, man. Next you'll be telling me you think he's *cute!*"

"Well, he is," Hayley admitted. "A little."

Whoa, Nelly. Had I heard right? Hayley "Hitler" Barker said I was cute? *And* a good mechanic? I leaned closer to the window so I could hear better.

It must've been the dust. Or maybe the decomposing hot dogs. Because suddenly, it happened.

My nose started to tickle.

And tingle.

And itch.

"*Ahhhh*-CHOOEY!"

"Your windmill is sneezing," Goldie observed.

Hayley's head appeared in the window. "What are *you* two doing here?" she demanded for the second time that day.

"Uh, just fixing the Windmill," I said, wiping at my nose.

"Without your tools?"

"It looked like an effortless job," Hiccup explained.

"Get out. *Now*."

Hiccup and I wriggled back into the sunlight.

"This is what we're paying you good money for?" Hayley asked. "To have you goofing off, spying on the customers, and—"

She stopped. Her mouth dropped open and her cheeks flushed three shades of pink.

Then she gulped and turned her squint on me, full force. "I told you I wouldn't let you get away with anything here, and I won't. You're—you're fired! And so is your friend!"

With that she spun around and ran down the path.

I started to go after her. "Hayley, wait! Let me explain!"

"Let her go," Goldie said, flipping her hair over one shoulder. "We have some business to discuss."

"I don't care. I *need* this job."

"I-know-about-the-bo-ok," Goldie sang.

"What book?" I asked casually, without turning around.

"*101 Ways to Bug Your Parents*. I was listening outside the bathroom window when you and Hiccup were talking about it."

Rats. I'd forgotten to check the window.

"Uh-(*hic*)-oh," Hiccup said.

"And I'm going to tell Scribbler," Goldie went on.

I turned to face her. "Who cares? I was going to tell him too. We have to get his approval at the topic conferences tomorrow, remember?"

Goldie crossed her arms. "But I bet you weren't going to tell him—or my mother, the Principal—about *selling* your book ... were you?"

I didn't answer.

Goldie tossed me a smug I-thought-so smile.

I sighed. "Okay, okay. What's the *information* you want?"

Her smile broadened. "I want you to find out—" she looked around to make sure no one was listening— "Ace's last name."

I almost laughed. "That's easy. It's ..." Hmmm. What *was* his last name?

"See? You don't know," Goldie said. "Nobody knows. Ever since kindergarten, he's always been Ace. Just plain Ace. Even Scribbler calls him that. And Scribbler calls *everybody* by their last name."

"Perhaps you should go directly to the source," suggested Hiccup.

"What?" Goldie asked.

"Ask ... Ace," he said, as if speaking to a one-year-old.

"Already tried that."

"And what did he say?"

"He didn't. He *yawned.*"

That was Ace. Cool to the core.

"But this morning when Scribbler was taking roll," Goldie went on, "I got a hint. Scribbler called Ace's name between Sherry Shahan's and Daniel Tanaka's. So his last name must begin with an *S* or a *T.* Betcha it's something really bizarre, like Shoppenoodle. Or Tablespoonski."

"Why do you care?" I asked. "I mean, what are you gonna do with this...*information* once you find out?"

Goldie tossed her head. "I'm not sure yet. I just want to *know.* Besides, he's saddled all of us with nicknames. Maybe it's time to give him one."

I sighed. I'd never much liked my nickname. Still, I'd never thought about seeking revenge for it.

"So, will you do it? Re-mem-ber," Goldie sang. "I-know-about-the-bo-ok."

"I'll see what I can do," I said. "Can't promise anything. But I'll try. Come on, Hiccup." I headed down the path.

"Hey, where are you guys going?" Goldie called.

"To get our jobs back," I said.

ELEVEN

You'd better wait outside," I warned Hiccup as we approached the office. "Maybe Hayley's had a chance to cool off. She might not get as steamed again if she sees only one of us."

My friend agreed with a hic and a nod.

I took a deep breath and pushed open the door.

Bad timing.

Hayley stood at the counter, hands on her hips, earrings swinging dangerously. She was arguing with two punks who had accidentally-on-purpose hit their golf balls into the pond. Now they were demanding their money back.

"Forget it," she said. "I saw what you did to hole number six. After you lost the balls, you tried to play with *doughnuts* instead. Two dozen of 'em. Now there are exploded doughnuts everywhere. And guess who's gonna have to clean them up? *Me.*"

"But I deserve something," the first punk whined. "After all, I shot a doughnut hole in one! Ha-ha! Get it?"

"Yeah, I get it," Hayley growled. She picked up a

putter and arced it over her head. "And you're gonna get it too, if you don't get out!"

The punks split.

"Ahem," I said. "Maybe I should come back later, when you're unarmed."

Hayley polished the putter and replaced it on the shelf. "What do *you* want? I thought I fired you."

"You did. I mean, you think you did, but I hope you didn't. I mean—"

I sighed. This was not going well. "Listen, Hayley, we're sorry. Hiccup and I weren't really goofing off. And we weren't spying on you. Honest. We just hid in the Windmill to get away from Goldie. She's been after me for days about something, and I—I didn't want to talk to her."

I looked straight into Hayley's ice-blue eyes. "It's the truth. You've met Goldie. You've *got* to understand."

"Huh," she said, although her usual squint eased open to half-mast.

"Please—give us a second chance. Hiccup and I are very hard workers. And there's lots of stuff you need done around here."

"Don't remind me." Hayley turned to sharpen a handful of scoring pencils. She ground away furiously on each. I winced, feeling like my own head was being whittled to a point.

At last she faced me again.

"You can't go around acting weird to the customers," she said, "even if you don't like them. You have to be friendly. And polite. See that sign? 'The customer is always right.'"

"But a second ago," I reminded her, "you were ready to bash two customers on the head!"

"Those hoodlums don't count. I mean *respectable* customers. We need them to have fun here. To come back and play golf again and again. Otherwise—" she swallowed—"*all* of us will be out of a job."

"Are things really that bad?"

"What do *you* think? You've worked at Gadabout three days now. How many golfers have you seen?"

I thought back. "Can I count the two punks who were just in here?"

"No."

"Well, then—none."

"Exactly. So go outside and act like a sweet baby bear to Goldie Laux, and maybe, just maybe, she'll decide to have her birthday party here."

"Does this mean we're not fired? That we get a second chance?"

"I'm not allowed to hire *or* fire," Hayley answered with a quick, smothered smile. "Only my dad can do that."

"Ah-*ha!*" I said. "You tricked me!"

"Yeah, but I *can* put you on probation. So watch your step. I'll be watching you." She concentrated on another bouquet of pencils. I guess that meant I was dismissed.

I headed for the door. Stopped. Turned back and walked around the counter to stand beside her. "Hey, did you mean it when you told Goldie that I'm a good mechanic?"

She shrugged. "Maybe. I don't know. Daddy says you are."

"Well, it's true. But I'm more than a mechanic. I'm an inventor. And I think I know how to make your golf course really cool so more people will want to come."

Hayley glanced up at me through a lock of hair. "Oh, yeah? How?"

"Well, your volcano, for example. I know how to make it burble and steam. I can even rig it to erupt with fake lava. And hole number fourteen, the Cemetery? I can make the tombstones dance up and down so it looks like ghosts are trying to escape."

"But all that costs money," she said. "And we don't have it."

"It won't cost that much," I argued. "I've learned how to do this stuff cheaply. Anyhow, sometimes you have to spend a little money to make money. At least that's what my friend Regan says."

She thought that one over. "I'll talk to Daddy about it. Now get back to work."

"Yessir!" I saluted. "And thanks." I started again for

the door. My hand jiggled the knob. "Um, one last thing." My face prickled hot. "Did you, um, really mean it when you ... um ..."

I paused, then blurted in one breath: "Didyoumeanitwhenyousaidlwascute?"

The only answer I heard was the grinding of pencils.

After work I bugged Mom and Dad for an hour to let Hiccup spend the night.

"Pleasepleasepleaseplease, puh-leeeeze?" I begged.

"What part of *no* don't you understand?" Mom said, kicking off her shoes and collapsing on the sofa. "I had a very frustrating day at the lab. And your dad taught three different classes at three different schools, and spent two hours stalled in rush-hour traffic. Plus he's got more papers to grade tonight. We're *tired*. We don't feel like having company."

"Hiccup's not company," Dad said from where he'd sunk into the depths of his overstuffed chair. "He's here so often, he's more like ... furniture."

"Whose side are you on?" Mom grumbled.

"Pleasepleaseplease?" I repeated.

"You heard your mother." Dad clicked open his briefcase, fanning papers across his lap. "Besides, it's a school night."

"I *know*. That's why I want Hiccup to stay over. We're anxious to start writing our books for school."

"Well, *this* is a switch," Mom said, perking up. She wiggled her stockinged toes at Dad. "See, I *told* you he'd like this class. He just had to give it a chance. So, what's your book about, honey?"

"Um, I'd rather not talk about it till it's finished," I answered. "It dilutes a writer's creative energy."

Dad nodded. "We understand."

"So can Hiccup stay over? Can he? Huh? Please-pleasepleaseplease?"

Mom sighed. "I'm honestly too tired to argue about it anymore, Steve. All right. He can come."

"Great!" I flung open the front door. "You can stay, Hiccup!"

Dad's eyes widened. "You mean he's been standing outside on the porch all this time?"

"Time is but a trifle," Hiccup said, "when the rewards are so great." He stumbled like a sleepwalker toward Mom, and handed her a test tube filled with water and one red rose. "For you."

"For me?" she asked, blushing. "How beautiful. Thank you, Hiccup."

"It's a science-and-nature motif," he explained.

"Yes, I can see that. Very thought-provoking. Thank you again."

"Let's go upstairs, Hiccup," I nudged.

"Huh?"

I thumbed toward the ceiling. "Up...stairs."

"Oh, yes, of course." He gazed dreamily at Mom. "Good-bye, Mrs. Wyatt," he said. "Until we meet again."

"Hoo, brother," I mumbled, and led the way to my room.

As Hiccup unrolled his hypoallergenic sleeping bag and fluffed up his special neck-support pillow, I added another suggestion to The List:

19. Beg them for things when they're really tired, until they say yes.

"Here's the plan for tomorrow, Hic," I said, opening my binder. "I'll set up shop in the boys' bathroom. I'll take orders for the book and collect money before school, at recess, and after school . . . before we go to Gadabout. You'll be in charge of crowd control. Keep the lines orderly. No pushing, cutting, or saving spots."

"Wait a moment," Hiccup fussed. "Did you say *lines*? No one has heard of your book yet."

"Goldie-the-Gossip has. Need I say more?"

"Ah, yes," my friend said with sudden understanding.

"Goldie's had most of the afternoon and all of tonight to call her friends, relatives, and mortal enemies," I went on. "We'll have so many kids crowding the halls looking for me, we'll need a traffic light. You'll act as sort of a school crossing guard, leading the masses safely to me."

I chewed the end of my pencil, thinking. "You'll also need to act as lookout. Make sure none of the teachers gets suspicious and comes to investigate."

"I can't be expected to stand for long periods of time," Hiccup protested. "I have phlebitis, you know. My legs will swell up and—"

"I'll get you a chair," I offered.

"That will be fine. What about the girls?"

"Let them get their own chairs."

Hiccup gave a double-hic of exasperation. "No, I mean, it is against school policy to allow girls in the boys' restroom. How will they place their orders?"

"Hmmm. I know! They can slip their orders through the window. Or maybe Goldie can collect them. Once she sees the crowds, she's gonna want to be in the center of all the excitement. I'll probably have to give her a job and a fancy title. Otherwise, she'll blab everything to her mother-the-Principal."

I drummed my fingers. "Okay, I've taken care of ordering, prices, money collection, supplies, and Goldie. Guess that's everything!" I slammed my binder down and took out my toolbox. The Nice Alarm needed a few minor tinkerings.

"I believe you've forgotten something of the utmost importance," Hiccup said. "The *book*."

"The book? What book?"

"*101 Ways to* (hic) *Bug Your Parents*. It's necessary to write it, remember?"

"Oh, that." I sprinkled food flakes into the aquarium. "Piece of cake, right, Ben? I've already thought up nighteen suggestions. That only leaves—"

"eighty-two to go," Hiccup finished for me.

"Ouch," I said. "That's a lot. How am I gonna come up with eighty-two more?"

Hiccup lay down on his sleeping bag, arms crossed beneath his head. "We must do it scientifically. As your mother once explained to me, science mostly involves undertaking an action or process designed to discover whether something is workable, effective, valid, etcetera."

"What?" I asked.

"We must gather, test, compare, analyze, and evaluate the data."

My mouth popped open and shut like Ben's. "In English, please."

Hiccup sighed. "It's very simple. Trial and error. We must experiment to see which are the *best* parent-bugging suggestions. If one is too weak, you will be ignored. Too strong, and you will be grounded. Or worse. Remember, there's a fine line between bugging and angering."

He flopped over, arms encircling the pillow. "You

don't want all your readers getting punished. They might demand their money back."

My stomach gave a squeeze of panic. "Oh, no. No refunds. We can't afford refunds!"

"Then you must make sure that each and every bugging suggestion works perfectly."

"How do we do that?"

Hiccup got to his feet. He stood in his Medicine Man stance: shoulders back, chin raised, an invisible cape snapping in the breeze behind him. "Sneeze, we must immediately embark on a marathon of bugging."

"What?"

"In the interest of science we must experiment on your parents."

He touched me on the arm, and his expression was one of extreme sadness. "Just promise me you won't be too hard," he said, "on *her*."

TWELVE

For the rest of that evening and at breakfast the next morning, Hiccup and I boldly bugged where no kids had bugged before.

We divided the results into three main categories: Duds, Dynamos, and Disasters.

Answering the phone in a silly voice was a Dud.

Calling to Mom, "Hey, toots, it's for you!" was a Dynamo.

Blurting out the surprise ending of the Monday Night Movie: a Dud. (Mom and Dad had seen it.)

Begging to stay up a half hour more, then another: a Dynamo. But when we begged for still *another*, it quickly turned to Disaster.

"Bed!" Dad shouted.

Wearing the same wrinkled clothes to school on Tuesday that I'd worn on Monday was a Dud. (No one noticed. Dad looks that way every day).

Telling Mom that ironing was a "woman's job" was a Dynamo.

Blowing bubbles in my cereal: Dud.

Laughing until milk squirted out my nose: Dynamo.

Telling Mom that science wasn't a "woman's job": definite crash-and-burn Disaster.

"*School!*" she shouted.

"It would seem that successful bugging requires a certain technique," Hiccup commented as we hustled onto the city bus. "Not only is it important *how* you bug, but *when*. Too many buggings lumped together in a short period of time renders them all ineffective."

I nabbed a seat and said, "I've noticed. I think with Mom and Dad we've reached CBM: Critical Bugging Mass. We should stop experimenting on them for a few days. Give them time to cool off."

Hiccup sighed with relief. He had closed his eyes and wince-hicked every time I'd scored a Dynamo with Mom.

"Then we must expand our research base," he said. "In other words, we must observe additional parent-child relationships in conflict."

"*What?*"

"We have to spy on other kids bugging their parents."

"Great idea. I still need seventy-one suggestions to complete the book. Spread out. We can eavesdrop on more people that way."

Hiccup agreed, and switched to another seat. By the time we got to school, we'd added three more items to The List. (*Pretend to barf. Ride with your feet out the window. Say 'I have to go to the bathroom' every five minutes.*)

We probably could've learned even more just standing in the parking lot while parents dropped off their kids, but we never got the chance.

Goldie was waiting.

"Where have you been?" she demanded, yanking my arm as soon as I stepped off the bus. She dragged me along behind her, blond hair whipping my face. "The natives are restless. Practically *everyone* in the upper grades wants a copy of your book."

I spit out a clump of her hair. "I don't have any copies yet, Goldie. I'm just taking orders for now. The book won't be ready for a couple of weeks." I pointed toward the boys' room. "I'm gonna set up, Hic. Spread the word, okay? Then meet me there ASAP."

He nodded, and trotted off.

"What can *I* do?" Goldie asked.

"Um, nothing right now. But thanks for offering. See ya—"

"I don't think," she warned, "that my mother, the Principal, would approve of this...."

Aha. Just as I'd hoped.

I pretended to look worried. "Well, um, I guess if I *have* to, I could give you a job, Goldie. How about . . . District Manager in charge of Special Orders and Purchasing?"

"Oooh, I *like* it." She rubbed her hands together. "Hey, wait a minute. Shouldn't I get a cut too? You know, a percentage of your profits."

"No way," I said. "But I *will* let you have . . . a free book."

"Deal!" Goldie shook my hand so hard, my whole arm jiggled like Jell-O. "I'll go drum up some Orderers and Purchasers!" she said, and sped away.

I borrowed a desk-chair combo from the storage room and dragged it into the bathroom, setting up at the far end underneath the open window. From my pack I took out a pen, notepad, and an old cash box I'd scrounged from our garage. I hoped everyone would have exact change. My 'cash' consisted only of three cents, two marbles, and a Barbie doll head.

Pierre rushed in moments later. "Am I zee first?" he asked. "How much is zee book?"

"Five bucks."

"Five!" He rolled his eyes. "Zees eez an outrage! How dare you take advanteege of zee friend in need!"

Friend? I thought. Since when was I his *friend*?

"Hey, you're the one who said you'd pay 'beeg' money for a list like this," I reminded. "And there will be 101—count 'em—*101* bugging suggestions. That's a bargain. So do you want to order a copy or not? If not, step aside. There are plenty of others who do." Six kids had already lined up behind him.

"Zees is what I call zee reep-off," Pierre said, "but I take two!" He shoved ten dollars into my hands. "One eez for my cousin. My aunt, she force zee poor boy to take zee tuba lessons!"

I wrote down the order and stashed the money in my cash box. "It's a pleasure doing business with you, Pierre. I'll let you know when the book's ready for delivery."

"Thank you, thank you!" Pierre kissed my hand. "We are all most grateful to our American lee-ber-a-tor!"

"Uh-huh," I said, wiping my hand on my jeans. "Next!"

The line had grown, snaking out the door. Boys thrust money at me, nickels, dimes, and quarters dug from the bottom of pockets, hidden in socks, or tied in plastic bags. Girls sent their money by airmail, white envelopes filled with dollar bills gliding like paper airplanes through the open window. By the time the first bell rang, I'd already made ninety—count 'em—*ninety* dollars.

"Sorry, everybody," I called to the kids still waiting. "I'm closing shop." I held up a hand to stop the groans. "I'll open again at recess. See you then!"

I packed up the cash box and pushed through the crowd. I met Hiccup and Goldie in the hall.

"Any problems?" I asked as we made our way to class.

"We experienced a close call," Hic said, still hicupping with the memory of his trauma. "Ms. McLoughlin saw the boys lined up outside the bathroom. She assumed they were sick, and wanted to page the school nurse about the epidemic."

I felt a twinge of panic. "Oh, man. What did you do?"

"I told her not to concern herself. That an anonymous person had written some graphic graffiti about acute coryza in stall number four, and we were all anxious to read it."

"Who's a cute core-iz-a?"

"Not *who*," Hiccup said, *"what*. It's the common cold!"

I laughed. "Nice save."

He beamed.

"My mother, the Principal," Goldie announced with importance, "would say that clogging the halls and blocking the bathroom door is a fire hazard. So as District Manager in charge of Special Orders and Purchasing, *I* say we need a better system. To cut down on traffic, there should only be five kids in the bathroom at a time. Maybe I can assign numbers or appointment times. I'll work on it."

"Thanks, Goldie," I said, opening the classroom door.

"No problem." She tugged on my sleeve, pulling me close enough to smell peanut butter toast on her breath. "Don't forget," she whispered, "about the... *information*. You might try sneaking a peek at Scribbler's attendance book."

I sighed but nodded. Goldie scuttled to her seat.

I smiled at Hayley as I passed her desk. She didn't smile back, but at least she didn't squint. Which, I hoped, meant our truce still held.

"Hey, it's Sneeze!" someone called.

"Morning, Sneeze," another voice said.

"Howzit goin', Sneeze ol' pal?"

Pierre patted the desk beside his. "Would you like to seet next to me? Zis desk has a good view of zee board."

Whoa, why was everyone being so friendly to me all of a sudden? They'd steered clear of me since kindergarten, afraid I'd sneeze on them—or worse. Even Ace arced an eyebrow and said, "Yo." And Ace was too cool to say "Yo" to anyone, even his own grandmother.

The final bell rang.

"All right, people," Scribbler said. "Take your seats quickly, please. We've got lots to do today."

A bunch of kids moaned.

Ignoring them, Scribbler went on, "You'll spend most of this morning in the school library, researching information for your books. I'll call you back to the classroom, one at a time, for the topic conferences. But first I want to talk about the importance of research. *Why* you need to do it, even if you're not writing a nonfiction book. And *how* to research, so you can find the best resources *fast*."

A bunch of kids groaned.

But I actually listened. I figured I needed all the help I could get. I mean, coming up with good ways to bug parents was harder than I'd thought. And I didn't exactly think I could log onto the library's computer system and find a book flashing on the screen titled *A Child's Guide to the Art of Parental Pestering*.

I was right.

Well, at least I wouldn't have to worry about competition. *101 Ways to Bug Your Parents* would be one-of-a-kind.

I glanced around the library to see if anyone else was having as much trouble with their research as I was. Nope. Pierre held a teetering tower of cookbooks. Hiccup riffled through four volumes of cartoons and comic strips. Only Hayley seemed lost. She stared into the other library computer, her face as blank as the screen.

I meandered over just as her fingers pecked out five letters.

"Need any help?" I asked.

She jumped, immediately hitting the delete key. But not before I saw the word she'd typed: *death*.

"Go away," she said, her voice flat.

I pretended not to hear. I mean, here sat a girl who supposedly thought I was cute. She couldn't *really* want me to go away ... could she?

"Go away," she repeated, still staring at the screen.

"Are you writing a nonfiction book about death?" I asked.

She caught her breath. After a few seconds she said, "No. I'm writing a story. What's it to you?"

"Just curious," I said, and sat down beside her. "What's your story about?"

"It's nothing." She shrugged. "It's—it's about a boy whose dad dies. He and his mom, they're left alone. And they miss him. And their lives are kinda rough."

A funny lump formed in my throat.

Write what's important to you, Scribbler had said. *Important to your life....*

I swallowed. The lump didn't budge. "Um, that sounds like a sad story." My words came out thick. "But interesting. You know. Powerful."

Hayley carefully tucked a curve of hair behind one ear. She still hadn't looked at me. "You think so?"

"Yeah, I do."

She shrugged again. "I don't know. Maybe. Maybe not. Maybe I'll just write about the history of the golf ball. Stuff like, why it has those little hollows all over it. They're called dimples, you know."

"The other book sounds more interesting."

Hayley frowned.

"Not that golf balls aren't interesting," I added. "They're, um, fascinating. And, um, white. Very white."

Hayley didn't answer, but her frown eased.

"So what happens to this kid and his mom? After the dad dies, I mean?"

"Well... the boy ... he has to take care of his mom a lot. 'Cause sometimes, his mom just isn't very smart. You know, about money and stuff."

"Oh. And how does it end?"

Hayley whispered, "I don't know yet...."

"Ah, Sneeze, zere you are," Pierre's voice interrupted from behind. He punched me lightly on the shoulder. "Eet eez your turn, my friend."

"My turn for what?"

"For what, he asks! To talk weeth Screebler, remembare? About zee book." He winked. "I 'ope, for all our sakes, that your book eez approved!"

"Yeah," I said. "Me too."

I felt a fist of anxiety tighten in my stomach. Scribbler had to okay my book. He *had* to. The Nice Alarm was at stake. But of course I couldn't tell him *that*. Especially knowing how he felt about my inventions.

"Why wouldn't it be approved?" Hayley's gaze had finally turned my way. Her eyes weren't cold anymore. Just cool and questioning. "What's your topic?"

"Um..."

"'Aven't you 'eard?" Pierre exclaimed. "Ah, our wonderboy Sneeze, he act, how you say, modest. But zee book, eet eez a masterpiece! 'E calls eet: *101 Ways to Bug zee Parents*."

Hayley's eyes frosted over again. She turned away. "What a stupid idea for a book," she said.

THIRTEEN

*W*hat a stupid idea for a book.

As I shuffled back to class, Hayley's words echoed in my mind as loudly as my footsteps in the deserted hall.

Why did she think it was stupid? Every other kid I mentioned the book to practically panted, drooled, or sat up and begged to get a copy. So why didn't Hayley?

You know why, a voice nagged. *That story she's writing—the one about the boy whose dad dies—it's really about . . . her.*

"It couldn't be," I said aloud.

Have you ever seen Hayley's mom around the golf course? the voice persisted. *Has she ever even mentioned her mom?*

No. But that didn't mean her mom was . . . *gone.* Maybe Mrs. Barker just didn't like golf. Or maybe Hayley liked writing sad stories.

Still, what if it was true? What would it be like to lose a mom or a dad?

My mom or dad?

I flashed back to the expressions on their faces during the Bugging Marathon. The memory gave me a funny hollow feeling in the pit of my stomach. I slurped a few gulps of water from the drinking fountain, but the emptiness didn't go away.

Maybe your book isn't such a great idea after all.

I hesitated, my hand clutching the doorknob of Room Seven.

But what about the Convention? How would I get there, how would the Nice Alarm have a chance if I didn't write the book?

I twisted the knob and went inside.

"There you are, Mr. Wyatt," Scribbler said. "I was just about to send out a search party. Come in, take a seat." He motioned to the metal chair across from his desk. "Now where did I put my pad?" He shuffled notes, peered under papers.

The attendance book lay open on top of the pile. I inched forward, trying to catch a glimpse of Ace's name. Rats. The book was upside down. Couldn't read a word. All the writing looked like Arabic.

"Here it is!" Scribbler whisked out his pad, pen poised. "So, Mr. Wyatt, what topic have you chosen?"

I jerked back from the attendance book, whacking my elbow on the hard chair. "Ow! Well, uh," I said, rubbing my arm, "it's an amusing topic...."

"Mm-hmm. Humor can be entertaining."

"And...it's instructive."

"Ah." He nodded. "A how-to book."

"Something like that. And . . . and it's unique. Never been done before. Like you said, 'Find a need and satisfy it.' Well, I think my readers will find it very satisfying."

Scribbler frowned over the top of his glasses. "Mister Wy-att."

I gulped. "Yes?"

"What *exactly* is your book about?"

Now or never. Do or die. I sat up straight and looked Scribbler right in the eye. "It's called . . . *101 Ways to Bug Your Parents*."

He didn't rant. He didn't rave. But his lips twitched at the corners of his mouth. "I see," he said, putting down his pen. "And what happened to the biography of Edison?"

I tried to choose my words with care. "It . . . uh, it didn't seem important enough. To me."

"And this other *topic* is?"

"*Very*." The word came out soft and solemn.

"Then please tell me more about it." He settled back in his chair. "I'm all ears."

I squirmed. "There's not much to tell. Um . . . it's a list. A list of things you can do when you feel like bugging your parents."

"What else do you know about this topic?" he grilled. "How will you research it?"

"I've self-tested a lot of the suggestions. And the

other ideas I've gotten from people I've spied on—I mean, observed."

Scribbler scribbled onto his notepad. "Now, how will you expand this? The title is a grabber, but to hold your audience the book *must* be more than a simple list. Will you dramatize any examples? Offer advice? Add personal commentary?"

I didn't answer. Why was Scribbler asking all these questions? It's not like he was really interested in the book. More like relieved. Relieved I wasn't writing something called *How to Invent an Atom Bomb in Your Classroom*. But that relief wouldn't last long.

Why didn't he get it over with? What was he waiting for? Why didn't he just say, "Ha! There's no way I'm approving your book!"

"Aren't you going to veto my book?" I blurted. "Aren't you going to tell me I have to write about something else?"

Scribbler leaned forward again. Pointed his pen at me. "Mr. Wyatt—"

The intercom squawked. "Mr. Powell," said Goldie's mother-the-Principal. "I need to talk with you. Could you come to my office for a moment?"

"Excuse me," the teacher said. "I'll be right back."

As the door closed behind him, I bit into a fingernail. Two questions bounced back and forth in my brain like a pinball. Would he? . . . *(Ding)* . . . or wouldn't he? *(Ding! Ding!)*

If he didn't approve my book, I could still write it. Still sell copies. But I'd have to write something else for class. When would I have time to do that? I wouldn't. Not with Gadabout, and getting ready for the Convention, and Goldie hounding me all the time.

Goldie. The attendance book.

If nothing else good came out of this conference, I could at least find out about Ace and finally get Goldie off my back.

I twirled the book to face me. Ran my finger down the list of names.

. . . Sherry Shahan . . . Daniel Tanaka . . . Stephen Wyatt.

Hmmm. Funny. Ace wasn't listed where Goldie said he should be.

Even funnier, Ace wasn't listed at all.

I checked the list again. Nope. According to this, he wasn't even enrolled in the class.

The door opened.

Scribbler!

Without thinking, I faked a great sneeze. A gargantuan twister of a sneeze. Papers scattered. Notes fluttered. I shoved the attendance book into the eye of the tornado.

"Sorry," I mumbled, sniffing. I started to scoop things back onto Scribbler's desk.

"Sit down, Mr. Wyatt. I'll straighten things later. By

the way, you haven't heard any rumors about graffiti in the boys' room, have you?"

I choked, and covered the noise with an intense nose-blowing session. "Uh, no."

"Never mind," Scribbler said. "Sorry about the interruption. Now, what were you saying?"

"The book. Are you going to veto it?"

The teacher adjusted his glasses and sighed. "Mr. Wyatt, this book belongs to you. I can't—and won't—tell you what you may or may not write about . . . *at home*. But I *am* responsible for what you write here at school. So before you begin, there are a few questions I need you to answer."

Here it comes . . .

"First," Scribbler said, "what do you want your readers to know at the end of the book? What do you want them to feel?

"Second, what's the most important thing you're trying to say with this book?

"Last but not least: Why is the book so important to you? In other words, why are you writing it?"

I started to speak.

He held up a hand. "No, no—don't say a word yet. I want you to think about these questions before answering them. And the answers aren't for me. They're for your ears only. With one exception."

Uh-oh.

"Your topic is a bit . . . ahem, different. I can't approve it until I'm satisfied you have a *very* good reason for writing it."

Double uh-oh.

"Well?" He tapped his pencil.

"Well..."

I'd have to tell him. For the Nice Alarm.

"I need money bad. And fast," I explained. "So I want to make copies of the book and sell it. To kids. For, um, money."

"And what do you need the money for?" Scribbler asked, doubt edging into his voice. "You're not going to tell me your mother needs an operation, are you?"

"No. But it's for something just as important. And...it's personal."

"I see." The teacher tapped his pencil again, then tossed it onto the desk. He glanced at his watch. "It's almost recess, Mr. Wyatt. You may go early if you like." He set about reorganizing the chaos I'd made of his desk.

"You mean," I said, "it's okay if I keep this topic?"

"I'm satisfied," Scribbler said simply.

"How'd we do?" Goldie asked, as she barged into the bathroom after school. "How many books did we sell today?"

"*Goldie*," Hiccup protested with an embarrassed hic. "This—this is the *boys'* room."

"Oh, pshaw," she replied, and hoisted herself onto a

sink where she sat, legs crossed. "Cut to the chase, Sneeze. How much did we take in?"

"*We* took thirty orders." I did some quick calculations, then recapped my pen. "Whoa! That means I've made one hundred and fifty dollars. Only a hundred bucks to go, and I'll have enough for the Convention deposit."

"You'll earn that *easy*," Goldie said. She handed me a sheet of binder paper. "I made you twelve appointments for tomorrow. And if I let my fingers do the walking—" she punched the numbers of an imaginary phone—"I *know* I can get you even more."

"Great. C'mon, Hiccup, let's clean up and clear out." I loaded the now-heavy cash box into my pack. "We've got to be at Gadabout in half an hour."

Goldie jumped off the sink. "I told Hayley I'd have my birthday party there," she said, "if—and only if—the place still doesn't look like the city dump."

"It won't," I said, my voice cool. "I've got big plans for it."

"And I'm supposed to believe you?" Goldie asked. "You haven't even followed through on the super easy stuff, like that *information* you owe me."

She scampered out of the bathroom after us, bumping into a boy going in. Confused, he looked at her, looked at the sign on the door, looked at her again, and ran off.

"Hey, just for the record," I said defensively, "I

checked Scribbler's attendance book. It doesn't list Ace's last name. Actually, it doesn't list Ace at all."

"Hmmm, that's strange." Goldie bit her lip. "His name must be something really bizarre not to be listed. You know, Spickleneedle. Tallyhogan. I guess you'll have to check his file in the master computer. It's in my mother the Principal's office. Lay low for a couple of days. I'll let you know when the coast is clear. See ya—"

"Wait—no. *Goldie!*" But she'd already darted off.

"Oh, great," I muttered. "Now she's going to get me arrested for breaking and entering."

"I don't understand," Hiccup said. "You're not considering a life of crime, are you?"

"Never mind, Hic. It's a long story." We trudged outside, heading for the bus stop.

"'Ello, Sneeze!" Pierre waved. He and a few other guys from class caught up with us. Ace sauntered after them.

"Hi, Sneeze, how's tricks?" someone said, giving me a high five.

Someone else patted my arm. "Way to go, Sneeze. Can't wait to see your book."

Even Ace gave me my second "Yo" of the day.

"You will join us for zee softball game, yes?" Pierre asked. "I like you for my team."

Wow. No one from class had ever asked me to play

ball with them before. No one from class had ever asked me to do *anything* with them before.

"Sorry, guys," I said. "Can't. Gotta work."

Pierre nodded. "Ah, work on zee book. We understand. But you must eat, no? You will join us at Dino's for pizza, after zee game. Zen we go to zee movies. We get good seats in zee balcony."

I couldn't believe my ears. "Sure! Sounds great. I'll have to check with my parents, but I'm sure it'll be okay."

"Good. Six o'clock. We meet you there, oui?" Pierre and his friends hurried off. Ace polished his fingernails on his shirt, then ambled after them.

"Wow," I said, this time aloud. "Pizza with Pierre. And *Ace*. I don't believe it! Hey, you're coming too, aren't you, Hiccup?"

My friend shook his head. "You know my lactose intolerance makes it impossible for me to partake of pizza."

"You could eat a salad."

Another shake of his head. "Sulfites. On the lettuce. They cause me to suffer paroxysms of wheezing."

"At least come to the movies with us," I pleaded.

"Balcony seats. Heights. Vertigo."

"Hiccup," I insisted. "Pierre and his friends have never, ever asked us to do stuff with them before.

Don't you know what this means? It means they don't think we're weeny little nerds anymore! They've accepted us. They *like* us!"

Hiccup scuffed his shoes against the sidewalk. "No. They like *you*."

"But, Hic—you're my best friend. I want you to come along."

"Thank you, but no. I'm not feeling very well today."

I picked up a stone and heaved it across the parking lot. "You're not really sick," I said, spitting out the words. "You make it all up! All your diseases and aches and pains—they're all fake! It's just an excuse not to do anything. Not to have any fun. Well, I'm the one who's sick now. Sick of you faking. Sick of *you*."

Hiccup stared at me, mouth open, the shock on his face a reflection of mine. His hiccups jerked out in a jumble.

I hung my head. "Oh, man. I didn't mean that—"

"Yes, you did. Good-bye, Sneeze." Hiccup whirled and started to walk away.

"Wait—where are you going? What about work?"

"I'm calling in sick. Oh, by the way . . ." he yelled over his shoulder, "your bedside manner (*hic!*) STINKS!"

FOURTEEN

Hiccup didn't come to school the next day.

Or the next day.

Or the next.

I called his house a couple of times. Over the noise of barking dogs and bickering brothers, his mom told me sorry, Hiccup was ill, couldn't come to the phone, good-bye. *Click.*

Couldn't come to the phone, I wondered . . . or *wouldn't*?

Maybe, for once, he was really sick. More likely, he just didn't want to be my friend anymore. Fine with me. Let him stay home with his buddies, Mr. Thermometer and Madam Stethoscope. I had new friends. Lots of them.

It was my dream come true, at last. Suddenly everybody in the upper grades knew my name. They waved and said "hi" to me in the hall. Patted my back. Shook my hand. Reached out to touch my sleeve when I passed, like I was magic and they hoped some would rub off on them.

Guys asked for my autograph. Girls asked me out. Pierre brought me fresh-baked pastries every morning. Only Hayley seemed not to notice my celebrity status.

Whenever I saw her at school or at Gadabout, she always gave me a blank nod, like my face seemed familiar, but she couldn't quite remember my name. Then she'd hunch over her notepad, filling page after page with her neat, rounded handwriting. Her arm curled over the paper like a fortress protecting her words, protecting her.

In a way, I kinda missed the old Squint of Suspicion days. At least then I knew *she* knew I was alive....

" ... two-forty-eight ... two-forty-nine ... two-hundred and fifty dollars."

On Friday afternoon Regan's eyes grew wide as I counted out the deposit money I owed him.

"Yes, yes, yes, yes, *yes*," he exclaimed. "Come to Papa!" He scooped the money into the register. "Sneeze, what'd you do, win the lottery? Where'd you get all this gravy?"

"Gravy?"

"Yeah, you know. Wampum. Greenbacks. Dead presidents. *Cash*."

"Oh." I laughed, and told him about my book. "It's selling like crazy, Regan. You wouldn't believe it! Sixty orders so far, and that's just to fifth and sixth graders. Next week I'm gonna spread the word to the rest of the school."

Regan scratched his head with a wrench. "Who would've guessed. You, a famous author! I figured you'd make the big time as an inventor, not a pen pusher."

"I'm still an inventor," I defended, "first and last."

"Hey, don't get testy with me, or I'll make you sleep in the motel bathtub. So what's on the drawing board now? Any new contraptions in the works?"

I felt an ache inside, like you do when you're hungry. Only this ache was inside my head. I was hungry for thinking.

"Too busy," I answered. "I've got school and work and now this book. And I haven't touched the Nice Alarm in days..."

My voice trailed off. I took a deep breath, filling my nose with the metal smell of nuts and bolts and confidence. The ache eased a little.

"But I'll get back to inventing soon," I insisted, more to convince myself than Regan. "And I'll have the rest of the money for you before we leave for the Convention. I promise."

After work Pierre and his friends treated me to another early dinner. We ate at Pierre's favorite restaurant, a pizazz-y pizzeria that serves pizza pies topped with—hold onto your stomach—*escargot*. (Pierre told me that's French for snails.)

"So, where eez zee book?" Pierre asked, popping

another rubbery-looking slug into his mouth. He licked garlic butter off his fingers with a smacking sound. "Eet eez almost fee-neeshed, oui?"

"Uh, no." I nibbled at a piece of pepperoni, feeling queasy. "I lost my . . . research assistant, so things are moving a little slowly. Don't worry. The book'll be done by the end of summer school."

"Zee *end* of school?" Pierre made a slashing gesture across his throat. "Zat eez com-pleet-lee un-acc-zep-ta-ble! We are tired of waiting. We need zee book *now*."

The pepperoni burned my throat. I took a sip of lemonade. "Uh, you mean *now* as in right this very second? Or now as in soon."

Pierre moved closer to me in the booth, his arm coming down hard across my shoulders. "Zee sooner zee better," he said.

I glanced around the table. Everyone nodded. Everyone except Ace, who was twisting straws into what looked like a hangman's noose.

I gulped. "Well . . . I guess I could try finishing my research this weekend, and type up The List Sunday night. I might be able to make copies of it Monday on the school photocopy machine, if the secretary says it's okay. So I could deliver it Tuesday at recess. Is that acc-zep—I mean, acceptable?"

"Eet eez good. We look forward to zee master-piece!" Pierre scooted out of the booth. The others followed him. Only Ace lagged behind.

"Hey, where you going?" I called. "I thought we might catch another movie."

"You 'ave work to do," Pierre said.

"But you could help," I protested. "We could hang out by the snack bar, spying on kids bugging their parents for hot dogs and popcorn. Or we could skip the movies and cruise the mall. There's gotta be a ton of families there on Friday night, and I bet the parents are really grouchy. We'll finish The List in no time. It'll be fun."

"Thanks, but no thanks." Pierre tilted his beret over one eye. *"Adios!"* He and his friends snaked away into the crowd.

"Adios isn't even French," I grumbled. "It's Spanish!"

With a sigh, I flicked a snail off my pizza slice and crunched into the last hunk of crust. If Hiccup were here, he wouldn't desert me. Except . . . he already had. At least when we were friends he never expected me to eat slimy animals that ooze across plants before they become someone's dinner.

I could feel eyes watching me as I chewed. I hoped they weren't a snail's. I glanced up. Ace hadn't left with the others. He stood lounging against the booth, waiting. Waiting for . . . me?

I leapt up. "Do *you* want to help?" I asked, my voice hopeful.

Ace tapped his chin and stared off into space, as if

giving it deep thought. For a second I believed he'd say yes. I think he *wanted* to say yes.

"Nah," he said at last. "I got things to do."

"What kind of things?"

He shrugged. "Things," he repeated, and ambled out the door.

Armed with notepad and pencil, I spent the rest of the weekend playing Undercover Boy. I spied, snooped, peered, pried, and eavesdropped on every kid-parent combo I could find, scribbling notes as fast as I could, then slipping away to tail the next unsuspecting subjects.

At a dressing room in the mall, I overheard an argument that became numbers sixty-two, sixty-six, and sixty-seven of The List. (*Leave chewed gum in the pockets of your pants, Wear jeans with holes in the knees, Don't wear the new clothes they buy you.*)

At a party in the park I witnessed number forty-three. (*Open your birthday presents, then say, "Is that* all?")

Observing a mom mumbling to herself in a pet store gave me number ninety. (*Take home the school rat for the whole summer.*)

And suppertime at my very own house provided me with a brand-new number one, two, and three. (*Slurp your dinner, Chew with your mouth open,* and *Burp with your mouth open.*)

"What is with you this evening?" Mom groused as

she cleared the dishes. "I've never seen you act so rude at the table. If you weren't our son, I'd swear you'd been raised in the wild by wolves."

"Huh?" I said. Number sixty-nine.

Mom shot a glance at Dad. "Honey, *please* say something to your son about the use of 'huh.' "

Dad looked up from the ever-present pile of students' papers and blinked. "Huh? Oh. Saying 'huh' is impolite, Steve. The proper term is 'pardon me.' "

"Huh?" I repeated.

Mom swatted me with a dish towel. "Why don't you go to Hiccup's for a while? I think we need a time-out from each other."

At the mention of my ex-friend's name, I got that funny hollow feeling in my stomach. Just a twinge, but it was the same emptiness I'd felt when I'd thought about losing Mom or Dad.

Time to face facts. I missed those *hic-hic-hics* in my ear all day long. Sure, they were annoying. But in a comforting way, like the monotonous chirping of crickets outside my window these warm summer nights. I really wished they'd stop so I could go to sleep. But the sound lets me know that all's right with the world. It's the moment they cut off into sudden silence that can be scary....

"Hiccup is sick," I told Mom. Sick of me, I thought. "And, um, we don't really have much time for each other anymore."

"You're with him all morning in school," Dad answered, "*and* after school. Or is he preoccupied more than usual studying diseases?"

"Hiccup not only studies diseases," I said, shredding my napkin into confetti. "He wants to *be* a disease."

"That would make sense," said Mom.

"Huh?"

"Don't say 'huh.' Try looking up his symptoms sometime. You'd be surprised to find they all add up."

Which symptoms? I wondered, sprinkling the confetti. There were so many.

"*What* are you doing to that napkin?" Mom demanded. "You're getting bits all over the floor! I think you'd better take that time-out up in your room. And *no* dessert for you tonight."

"Hey, no fair! You're treating me like a little kid!"

"That's because you're acting like one," Dad said. "Now scoot."

"But, Dad—"

"Go!"

"But, Mom—"

"Go!"

I went. But not before giving them a taste of number 101 on The List: *When you don't get your way, sulk, cry, or whine.*

FIFTEEN

Hiccup returned to school on Tuesday.

I was so happy to see him, I forgot we were supposed to be mad at each other.

But *he* hadn't forgotten.

"Hey, Hic!" I said, clapping him on the shoulder. I thunked my overweighted pack onto my desk and sat down. "How you feeling?"

"What do you care?" he answered, his voice frosty. He didn't bother to look up from his research books.

"Brrr," said Goldie. "Sure is nippy in here."

"I'll say," I muttered. I wished Hiccup would yell at me. Cuss and shout and wave his arms. Maybe throw a book or two. Anything would be better than the cold shoulder.

I tried again.

"Um, I called your house a few times—" I began. Then I noticed his face. In between the freckles, it was covered with scabs and faded pink blotches.

"Whoa, what happened to you?" I leaned sideways to get a better view.

He turned a page before deciding to answer. "Varicella."

"What's that?"

"Chicken pox. And *no*—" he whirled toward Goldie, "it is not a chicken disease."

Her cheeks turned as pink as Hiccup's scars. "I *know*," she snapped, and flounced away.

"So, um ... you really *were* sick," I said.

Hiccup finally fixed his gaze on me. Dark smudges encircled his eyes. His face looked pale beneath the scars.

"What—did—you—think?" Icicles hung from his words.

"Nothing." I mumbled. "Nothing." I felt bad for not believing him. And yet, how was I supposed to know *this* time was for real?

Try looking up his symptoms sometime, Mom had said. *You'd be surprised to find they all add up.*

What had she meant?

The final bell rang. Hayley scrambled in at the last minute, notepad in hand, Pierre on her heels.

Scribbler started to take attendance.

"Psst—Sneeze." Pierre leaned across the aisle. "Did you feenesh eet? Did you bring eet?"

I didn't have to ask what 'eet' was. I pointed to my bulging pack and gave him a thumbs-up.

"*Magnifique!*" he cried out. Then clapped his hand over his mouth, eyes wide.

The room echoed with stunned silence.

Using a finger to mark his place in the roll book,

Scribbler fixed Pierre with a frown-down-over-his-glasses look. "Is there a problem, Mr. Noel?"

Pierre gave a nervous laugh. "Ah, no, so sorry. I am overcome for zee moment, but, uh, I am all right now."

"Glad to hear it," Scribbler said. "I hope to find your cookbook as magnificent as you seem to find roll taking."

A few kids snickered.

Pierre hunched into his shirt collar. But he whispered, his lips barely moving: "Ree-cess. Boys' room. Ten o'clock. We come for zee books, oui?"

"Oui," I agreed. "Spread the word."

He began whispering to some of the other kids.

I wondered if Hiccup could hear. Did he feel guilty that I'd slaved without his help to make all those sales? Was he jealous I'd finished my book three weeks early, while he'd barely begun his research?

And the biggest question of all: Was he dying to catch a glimpse of The List?

I pulled a copy from my pack, edging it casually to the corner of my desk.

Was he tempted?

I sneaked a peek.

Our eyes met. Locked. Hiccup blinked. Hicked.

Then slowly, deliberately, he shifted in his seat, turning his back on me.

When I reached the bathroom at recess, a crowd of

boys already stood waiting three-deep. They jostled and punched each other with excitement. From the sound of higher-pitched chatter and laughter floating into the room, I knew that a line of girls had formed outside under the open window.

I handed Goldie a stack of The List. "Pass them out fast," I said, "before a teacher notices these lines. Don't forget to make sure each person paid, and check their names off the order form."

"I know, I know," she responded in a huff. "I'm the District Manager in charge of Special Orders and Purchasing. I created this system, remember?"

Still, she snatched the stack from my hands and positioned herself beneath the window. "Pipe down out there," she ordered, "or my mother, the Principal, will see you get detention."

I settled into my chair.

"Hur-ry, hur-ry, hur-ry!" I called like a carnival barker. "Step right up! Sneeze Publishing is open for business."

Pierre, of course, was first in line. He rubbed his hands and said, "Ah, I 'ave waited so long for zis moment!"

"Well, here you go!" I checked off his name. "That's one copy for you, and one copy for your cousin-the-tuba-player. Let's keep this line moving. Next!"

Pierre didn't budge. He stared at the photocopied pages I'd handed him. Probably admiring the nifty cover, I thought. I'd used eye-catching red construction paper.

"Ha-ha," he said at last. "Ver-ree fun-nee. Now where eez zee real book?"

"What do you mean?" I asked.

"Do you not speek Eengleesh? There must be some mees-stake. You 'ave given me what Screebler call zee rough draft. I would like zee copy of zee real book, please."

"Zis—I mean, this *is* the real book."

Pierre wrinkled his nose. He dangled The List by one corner, like it was a dirty diaper. "I pay five American dollars for *zis*? I don't zink so!"

"What's going on up there?" a boy called from the back of the line.

"Yeah, let's get this show moving."

"I gotta go to the bathroom!"

I cleared my throat. Lowered my voice. "Um, what's the problem, Pierre?"

"Zee problem is, I pay for a *book*. Do I get a book? No! I get a leest. A measly ten-page leest wis a stapled cover. Eet look like something my leetle brothare make! And 'e eez only three!"

I jerked back my chair. "Hey, I resent that! I spent a lot of time putting this list together. Besides, it's not how it looks that counts. It's what's inside that's important. You want to know how to bug your parents? Well, right here I've given you 101 ways for doing it!"

"Zat ees not enough," Pierre insisted. "I do not pay five dollars for a book I can read in five minutes. I want something *more*. Something, how you say, wis more meat."

"Yeah, yeah," a few kids echoed. "Meat."

Pierre raised his voice and addressed the crowd. "I suppose we should 'ave expected zis, no? All Sneeze's inventions are failures. Why did we think zis time would be dee-fer-ent?"

The crowd murmured and nodded.

"Oh-oh," Goldie said behind me.

Pierre put his hand out, palm up. "So. You will return my money, oui?"

"What?!" I sank low into my seat. "You want a . . ." the word came out an agonized whisper, *"refund?"*

"Oui, please. Now, please."

"Same here!" a voice called.

"Yeah, me too!"

"Me three!"

"So do we!" chorused the girls outside.

I gulped. "But—but the money is gone. I spent it. . . ."

"Zat eez your problem," Pierre said. "And there eez only one solution. You will write a bigger book. A better book. Or, you refund our money. *All* of eet."

"Okay, okay." I wiped a trickle of sweat from my forehead. "I'll revise the book. I promise. But that's gonna take time. I'll need at least a couple of weeks. Maybe till the end of school."

"Zees eez an outrage!" Pierre shook his fists at the ceiling.

"Oh-oh," Goldie repeated. She zipped into the nearest stall and locked the door.

Pierre whipped off his beret. He waved it in front of the crowd like a conductor's baton. "We-want-zee-money-back," he began to chant. "We-want-zee-money-back."

The crowd pressed forward and echoed, "We want our money back."

"Pierre!" I squeaked. "What are you doing? I—I thought we were friends."

"HA!" His chanting grew louder. "We-want-zee money-back!"

"We-want-our-money-back!"

The crowd closed in around me. Their faces seemed to expand and distort, like twisted balloons.

I squeezed my eyes shut.

This is it, I thought. My life is over. I could see the headlines now: *Boy-Inventor's Dreams of Success Flushed Away in Restroom Tragedy.*

They pushed closer....

"We-want-"

Closer...

"our-money-back!"

Then I heard a calm "Yo."

Instantly the room fell silent.

I cracked open one eye.

Ace.

He stood in front of me. Not to fight me. To *protect* me. "Be cool," he drawled to the mob. "Sneeze will finish the book as fast as he can ... won't you, Sneeze?"

I could only nod. My tongue had glued itself to the roof of my mouth.

"Humph," Pierre said. But he tugged his beret back onto his head. "You better feeneesh eet," he added. "Or we invent 101 ways to bug *you*, oui?"

He stalked out of the bathroom.

The crowd stared at me. The faces had shrunk again. Now they looked like normal faces. Kid faces.

Mumbling and grumbling the boys broke ranks and followed Pierre out the door. Ace flicked a speck of lint from his shirt, then ambled after them.

Goldie inched out of the stall. "Boy, that was close."

"I'll say." My whole body felt wobbly. Cold. Yet my face was hot. I wanted to ooze down onto the floor and rest my cheek against the cool tiles.

But there was something I had to do first.

I pushed out of my chair and stumbled into the hall.

"Ace!" I called. "Ace—wait up!"

He stopped, turned, arced one eyebrow.

"Thanks," I said. "Thanks for saving my life."

He shrugged, as if rescuing people came naturally, like breathing.

"Just get that book revised," he warned. "And fast."

SIXTEEN

I know most of you are still 'baking' the rough drafts of your books," Scribbler said after recess. "But soon you'll need to add the final and most important ingredient. I'm talking about—" he paused to chalk eight letters on the board— "the *revision*."

I straightened in my seat and uncapped my pen. Hooray, I'm saved, I thought. Scribbler is a writer. He, more than anyone, will know a fast way to fix my book. I'll bet he even has an easy check-off list.

I numbered my paper from one to five, just in case.

"Vision means 'to see,'" the teacher went on. "So *re*-vision means to see something again. Now tell me: If your story is finished, why would you want to look at it again?"

Pierre raised his hand. "To feex zee spelling or zee grammar. Or—" he jerked his beret toward me—"to feex zee *millions* of othare meestakes."

My hair prickled.

"That's only a small part of it, Mr. Noel," Scribbler said. "Often people think of revisions as fixing what they've done wrong. But I like to think of them as taking something good . . . and making it better. Making your book the *best*."

I nodded. Okay, Scribbler, I thought. I'm ready anytime you are. Just tell me what to do. . . .

"I recommend that you ask someone to read your rough draft and comment on it," the teacher continued. "This person will tell you what he or she likes about the book, and what problems he or she has with it. Often we get too close to our work. We like it so much, we don't notice when a thought is unclear or a sentence is boring. Or when an idea isn't fully developed."

Scribbler took off his glasses and leaned forward. "The key is to pick someone you can trust. Someone who will give you an honest, constructive opinion."

His next words sounded like an open hand, ready to clasp ours and lead us to safety. "I hope some of you will feel free to choose *me*. I would love to read your books."

He sat quiet for a moment, letting his words sink in. Then he slid on his glasses again. "Okay, people. Back to work!"

Papers rustled and binders snapped as everyone pulled out their manuscripts.

That's it? I thought, staring down at the blank spaces on my paper. That's Scribbler's helpful revision tip for the day: Get someone's honest opinion?

Hey, I'd already gotten one of those from Pierre and his friends. Fix the book—or else.

I gulped. Maybe I just needed to find another reader. Preferably someone I didn't owe money to. But who? Who would take the time to read my book and offer suggestions to make it better? To make it the *best*?

Not Hayley. She didn't like my topic.

Not Hiccup. He didn't like *me*. Not anymore.

Mom and Dad? As always, they were too busy with their own work to worry about mine. Besides, one look at the title and Mom would start making her cow noises.

That left... Scribbler.

I thought back to what he'd said and how he'd said it. *I would love to read your books.* He sounded so sincere. But he couldn't mean *my* book. He'd never liked anything I'd done. Why should now be different? To him, this book would only be another of my failed inventions....

If I wanted *101 Ways to Bug Your Parents* revised, I'd have to do it on my own.

I just didn't have a clue how.

After school I headed straight to Gadabout, even though I wasn't scheduled to work that day. It sounds strange, but whenever a problem clutters my head, thinking out an invention sweeps up the cobwebs so that I get a better view. And I had a great idea for a new invention. An invention that was perfect for hole number eighteen, the Pirate Ship.

"What are *you* doing here?"

"Huh?" I looked up, blinking. I'd been sitting on board so long, tinkering with my new project, I'd almost forgotten where and who I was.

"What are *you* doing here?" Hayley repeated. She towered over me, blotting out the sun. The Squint of Suspicion had returned at last. Seeing it made me want to hum with contentment. Like whenever I ride past the fast-food restaurant Tubby Burger.

When I was six, Mom and Dad took me on our one-and-only family vacation: a three-week driving trip across the country. I'd wanted to stop and eat at every single Tubby Burger in every single town we drove through, even though their burgers tasted like grilled dirty socks—with pickles. They'd tasted the same way at our Tubby Burger at home. To a homesick kid, that was somehow reassuring.

And so was Hayley's squint. It was expected. *Normal*. Not like my life the last couple of days.

"I work here, remember?" I finally answered.

Hayley waved a time card in my face. "You've already worked more hours this week than you're allowed."

"Yeah, I know. But look what I've designed! I call it the Golf Gopher. You're always having problems with people not returning balls after a game, right? Well, now they'll return themselves! Come on, I'll show you."

I grabbed my pack and we thumped down the gangplank. I sketched a picture on my notepad, then pointed at the ship.

"See, instead of aiming for that hole on deck, the golfer hits the ball into the mouth of the cannon. The ball will plop out the other end and scurry along a tunnel leading to the main office. As it rolls, it gets doused with jetsprays of water, and air-dried. Then it zips up to a slot at the check-in counter, all clean and polished and eager for another round! Cool, huh?"

Hayley squinted closer at my sketch. "Hmmm, yeah. It'll save me a lot of work. I won't have to leave the counter unattended to hunt down golfers who—hey, hold on a minute! I told you, you're not supposed to be here. I'm not allowed to pay you."

"That's okay." I glanced around. "Now, where did I leave my toolbox?"

Hayley crossed her arms. "You're doing this because you feel sorry for me, aren't you?" she demanded.

"Huh?"

"Well, I don't want or need your pity. So just go on home."

"What are you talking about?"

"Don't play dumb. The story I'm writing. The one I

mentioned that day in the library. You guessed that it's really about..." her voice dropped low and rough, "me."

I kicked at a ragged piece of AstroTurf. "I thought so," I admitted, not looking at her. "But—but if it makes you feel better, I'm *not* building the Golf Gopher for you. Honest. I'm—I'm building it for *me*."

Hayley doubled the strength of her Squint. "That's crazy. Why would you do that?"

Why? I rocked back on my heels. I'd never before thought about the *why* behind my inventions.

"Because . . ." I hunkered down to think. "Because inventing is what I *do*. I mean, sure it'd be nice to get paid for it. But I'd only use the extra money to buy stuff for more inventions."

I waved my time card. "See, when I design a new contraption, and I build it and test it and rebuild it and test it again and it *works*. . . the feeling I get inside is exactly like getting paid. Only better."

Hayley sat in the plastic grass beside me. She gazed out at the Windmill's colorful sails spinning lazily in the breeze, like a giant pinwheel in slow motion.

"Yeah, I know," she said, the words soft as the breeze. "I feel the same way about working here. That's why I don't want to lose it."

"Is it really going under?" I asked. "I mean, I know business is bad, but—"

"Bad?" Hayley said. "It's *awful*. Not like in the old

days. I remember when Gadabout used to be packed every weekend. Every night..."

"So what happened?"

She swallowed. "Mom died, that's what happened. And—and everything fell apart."

I didn't know what to say. I just nodded and waited for Hayley to go on.

After a minute she said, "See, Mom and Daddy used to run Gadabout together. She did the business stuff; he took care of the golf course. They loved this funky place. I remember hearing them late at night, talking and laughing, dreaming up new ideas for the course. Like the Giant Swiss Cheese. Did you know that if you hit a hole in one, a mouse skitters up the flag and squeaks at you? That was Mom's idea. And Daddy built it."

"I didn't know," I said. "That's neat."

Hayley nodded. "They were a good team. Then ... Mom died and it ... it was like Daddy died too. He walked around like a zombie. He didn't care about anything anymore. Not even Gadabout. He let the place get run down. So people stopped coming. That was two years ago."

Loose strands of Hayley's hair blew across her face. She urged them behind her ear.

"He's better now," she continued. "We've worked together to fix up this place. It's been fun. Almost like the old days...."

A smile tugged at her lips, then faded.

"But it's too late. The people haven't come back. Oh, they dribble in. But when they do, Daddy's so happy to see them, he lets them walk all over him. Always letting little kids in for free, or paying hoodlums twenty-five cents apiece to scoop balls out of the pond that *they* threw there. Or hiring workers we can't afford."

I coughed.

"Oh. Sorry," Hayley said, the tip of her nose turning pink. "But at least you know what you're doing. You've really fixed stuff around here. Huh. Smartest thing Daddy ever did was hiring you. He's *helpless* when it comes to business stuff. I have to keep an eye on him all the time, and that bugs me. I mean, he's a parent. He's supposed to know these things, isn't he?"

I didn't say anything. I got the feeling Hayley didn't expect an answer. Like she was talking to herself.

After a while I asked, "How did your mom die?"

"Car accident." Hayley ripped out a blade of grass. "When I went to play at a friend's one morning, she was here. When I came back in the afternoon, she was . . . gone. Just like that." She snapped her fingers. "Daddy says I need to spend time away from Gadabout. Make new friends and have fun and stuff. But what if the same thing happens again? What if I come home one day and . . . and he isn't here anymore?"

I remembered the funny hollow feeling I'd got when I thought about losing Mom or Dad.

"It must feel like a hole," I said slowly. "A hole inside you somewhere that you can't fill up again. At least, not the same way."

Hayley turned to stare at me. Her eyes glistened. "That's *exactly* how it feels," she said. "How did you know?"

I shook my head. I didn't want to tell her I had a tiny hole of my own. A hole where Hiccup used to be.

"Would you . . ." Hayley began, then stopped. She took a deep breath and began again. "Would you read my story? The one about my mom?"

I touched my chest. "Me? You want *me* to read it?"

"Never mind. Forget it." Hayley rose to her feet.

"No, no. I'll read it if you want me to. I mean, I *want* to. But why me?"

Hayley folded her arms again, like she was protecting herself. "Mr. Powell told us we should pick someone we trust," she said. "And I trust you to be tough. I don't want someone who's gonna read this and get all weepy on me. Or feel sorry for me. When I finish the revision, I want people to like this story because it's good. Not because I don't have a mom."

I thought that one over. "I'm not a very good writer," I said, "but I'd like to read your story. And I'll help you make it better, if I can. On one condition."

Hayley snorted. "No, you *can't* have a raise."

147

I laughed and shook my head. "Not that. The condition is: I'll read your book if—if you read mine." I pulled a copy of The List from my pack and held it out to her.

"I don't like your topic," she warned.

"That'll help you to be tough," I replied.

Hayley took The List from my hand. "Okay," she said. "You asked for it."

SEVENTEEN

Hayley glanced down at The List and took a few steps toward the office.

"But this is—" she stopped. Cocked her head. Stared at The List for a long time.

Then she *chuckled*.

I'd never heard her do that before. It sounded musical, like water tripping over rocks and reeds in a stream.

"This is *funny*," she said, incredulous. "I thought you were writing it to be mean, but you're not! You're trying to make kids *laugh* at the things they do to their parents. I didn't know you were so clever!"

"I am?"

"Uh-huh. And you grab your readers right away, just like Mr. Powell told us to!"

"I do?"

"Sure. Because you know exactly how your readers feel. How *I* feel. I mean, sometimes when Daddy spends too much money and he won't listen to me, it bugs me so much I want to *scream*. Now, instead, I can read about doing number ninety . . . or number twenty-one . . . or—" she laughed— "number seventy-seven."

"So you like it?"

She laughed again, the golf-ball earrings swinging. "Yeah, I do."

"Enough to pay five bucks for it?"

The Squint returned. "What do you mean?" she asked suspiciously.

I told Hayley about the Convention. My desperate plan to get there. And what had happened that afternoon in the boys' room.

"No wonder Pierre's so mad," she said. "Your list is great, but that's all it is: a list. If you want it to be a great *book*, you've got to do more."

"So everyone tells me. But what? How?"

"Come with me to the office," Hayley said, "and we'll brainstorm."

Along the way, she bought two Cokes from the soda machine. We spritzed them open, then perched on stools at the main counter.

"I see your problem," Hayley said. She sipped her Coke and scanned the rest of The List. "Mr. Powell always says, 'Show, don't tell.' But you're doing the opposite. You're *telling* the readers what they can do to bug their parents, but we don't really *see* the suggestions. Know what I mean?"

I shook my head.

"You should write each suggestion like a scene in a

play," she explained. "You know, invent a kid character and describe him bugging his parents like it's happening *right now*. Write what they say and do. And ..." she fingered an earring. "And how the parents look with steam bursting out of their ears!"

I faked a groan. "My mom and dad have looked like that a lot lately. I'm surprised they haven't grounded me. Or worse."

"I never thought of that," Hayley said. "See, that's something else you could do! Point out the dangers of your list. Like: *Warning! These suggestions may be hazardous to your health!*"

"Good idea." I jotted it down on my notepad. "When Hiccup and I did our research, we learned there's a fine line between bugging your parents and making them furious." I chewed the end of my eraser. "So ... maybe I should recommend the best and worst bugging times."

"Yeah!" Hayley agreed. "You could say: *Never use all the hot water for the shower when your dad's late for an important meeting.*"

"I like that," I said, jotting more notes. "Now look at number nine: *Laugh with a mouthful of milk until some squirts out your nose.* I could say it's okay to do that at home, but *never* when you're having dinner with the President of the United States."

"Maybe with just the Principal," Hayley added, and we laughed.

Then I thought of something not-so-funny.

"The only problem with these ideas," I said, "is they're going to make my book longer. It could end up being a hundred pages! That means I'll need more paper. And a stiffer cover to hold the pages together. That's gonna cut into my profits, big time. Which means..."

The next words hurt. "Which means I won't have enough money for the Invention Convention."

I propped my chin against my hands and sighed.

"There's only one solution then," Hayley said matter-of-factly. "You'll have to sell more books."

"I know. But most of the upper graders have already bought one. I need an incentive. A gimmick to make them want to buy another copy. A reason to tell their *friends* to buy copies. But what?"

I stared out at the deserted golf course, my mind racing.

And that's when my nose started to tickle.

And tingle.

And itch.

Only this time it wasn't a sneeze brewing in my head. It was an idea. An idea so brilliant, I had to close my eyes to ward off its shine.

"I'll offer a coupon with each book," I said, trying to keep my voice calm. "A two-dollars-off coupon for a game of Gadabout Golf."

"What?!" Hayley leapt up. "I can't believe you'd

take advantage of Daddy—of me!—like this. Not after he gave you this job. Not after—"

I grabbed her arm. "Calm down! I'm not taking advantage of anybody. Store owners do this all the time. They offer people a discount, which gets more customers into the store. The people like the store so much, they come back again and again. That's what'll happen here. Kids will see that Gadabout has changed. That it's like the old days. They'll start coming back. And they'll tell their friends—"

"But two whole dollars off!" Hayley gave a low whistle. "We can't afford to do it."

"You can't afford *not* to," I said. "And I can't either. Besides, sometimes you have to spend money—"

"to make money," Hayley finished.

"Uh-huh." I smiled, pleased that she'd remembered.

Hayley glanced at the financial ledger sitting on the counter. She shoved it into a drawer. "There's probably an old gift certificate lying around in the supply room," she said. "I could make a sample coupon out of that. Could you photocopy it at school?"

"Sure. At recess tomorrow."

She took a deep breath. "Then let's go for it. Deal?" She stuck out her hand to shake.

"Deal." Her fingers felt cool. But for some weird reason, they made mine grow warm.

Hayley stared into my eyes with a squint I'd never seen before. Then she looked away, and headed for the supply room.

"Hold on," I ordered. "You're not doing this 'cause you feel sorry for me, are you? I mean, about the Convention. Because if you are, forget it. Deal's off."

Hayley's chin jerked up. "I'm doing it for *me*. And for Gadabout."

"Well, okay, then." I stuck out my hand. "*Now* we have a deal."

We shook again, holding hands just a bit longer than we needed to.

"And," Hayley added, fast and low, "becauseI-thinkyou'rereallycute."

"What?" I asked. "What'd you say?"

But she had already hurried off.

"Ah-ha! I knew I'd find you in here," Goldie said the next day at recess. She bustled into the staff room, where I was just about to flip on the photocopy machine. "Let's see Hayley's coupon."

"How do you know about the coupon?" I asked. "And how did you know where I'd be?"

"Oh, I have my spies," she answered. "Besides, it's my business to know. Now hand over that coupon." She whipped it out of the machine. "Hm. Not bad. Not bad at all."

"I think it's great." I plucked it from her hands and

carefully repositioned it for copying. The coupon had fancy curlicues decorating its edges, and two golf clubs crossed like swords in each of the four corners. In proud, bold lettering it read:

THIS CERTIFIES
THAT BEARER IS ENTITLED TO
$2 OFF ONE GAME OF GADABOUT GOLF.
OFFICIAL SIGNATURE: _____
EXPIRATION DATE: *August 31st.*

The last line was an ingenious touch, I thought. Hayley was determined to get crowds of customers into Gadabout as quickly as possible.

I set the machine for one hundred copies, the way the receptionist had shown me, and pressed Start.

"Okay, hurry up, gotta go," Goldie said, looking over her shoulder and tugging on my arm at the same time.

"Go? Where are we going?"

"Not *we. You.*" She opened the door of the next office, and shoved me inside.

I glanced around. A normal office. Desk. Phone. File cabinet. Framed photo of Goldie and her mother-the-Principal.

Goldie and her mother . . .

"Whoa—wait a minute!" I said, backing up. "What are we doing in here?"

"You still owe me that *information*," she said. "Or had you forgotten?"

I groaned. "Yes. And I was hoping you had too. C'mon, Goldie, can't you just leave Ace alone?"

"No. I've *got* to know his last name. I'll bet it's something *horrifying*." She gave me another shove. "There's the master computer, on her desk. Just type in the code word *Goldilocks* and you'll be in the student files. Easy as pie."

"If it's so easy, why don't you do it?" I asked.

"Because my mother, the Principal, is in the conference room down the hall, and somebody's got to keep her busy. Do *you* want to do that?"

"Not exactly."

"That's what I thought. Now hurry."

"May I ask what you two are doing in here?" a voice demanded behind us.

I whirled around. Put my hands up. "Don't shoot!" I said.

Hiccup stared at me and blinked.

Goldie let out a dramatic sigh. "Oh, it's only *you*. What do you want?"

"I am in search of the nurse," he explained. "It's time for my dose of antipruritus medication."

Goldie edged closer to me. "What's *that*?"

He scratched at a chicken-pox scab on his forehead. "Anti-itching cream."

"Oh. Well, I'm fresh out." She threw me a glance.

"Get that information, Sneeze, and get it *now*. I don't know how long I can keep Mother busy."

She elbowed past Hiccup and slammed the door.

I gazed nervously at the computer keyboard and rubbed my fingertips. *Easy as pie*, Goldie had said.

Yeah, easy as getting arrested.

But which was worse? Jail, or Goldie hounding me till the end of my days, saying I owed her *information*?

Goldie. No contest.

My hands inched forward....

But what Goldie asked you to do is wrong, said that little voice inside my head.

Yeah, I know.

Besides, maybe Ace has a reason for not telling anyone his last name. If he wants it kept secret, you should respect his privacy....

I shoved my hands into my pockets and stepped away from the computer.

I couldn't do it. *Wouldn't* do it.

Hiccup still stood there. "Do all your new friends order you around like that?" he asked. "Or are you only on Goldie's leash?"

"What do you care?" I shot back.

"I don't," he answered, turning to go.

"Wait. Stop, Hiccup. I didn't mean to say that."

"What did you mean to say?"

"I don't know. I—"

Just then we heard Goldie's voice.

And her mother-the-Principal's.

In the staff room . . .

"But, Mother," Goldie said in a desperate whine, "I need you to come look at something *right now*!"

"Later, sweetness. I have to make an important call."

. . . coming this way.

"Hide!" I whispered hoarsely at Hiccup.

We tried to run. Bounced into each other. Jerked around. No place to go. No place to hide....

Trapped.

EIGHTEEN

"But *Mother*—" Goldie pleaded.

The door started to open.

In the last seconds, I yanked Hiccup's arm and we squeezed together under the Principal's desk. Then I reached out and rolled the chair in front for cover.

"*Hic!*" Hiccup said.

I clapped a hand over his mouth. "Don't," I mouthed.

Wide-eyed, he nodded.

Tap-tap-tap-tap.

From my scrunched position, I could see the Principal's high heels spike across the floor toward the desk. Goldie's red, sequined sneakers squeaked close behind.

Please don't sit down, I thought. Please...

"Mo-ther, it's re-ally im-por-tant," Goldie begged. "Come *on*."

"Honey, don't tug on my sleeve like that. You'll wrinkle my blouse."

"Mo-ther—"

"I have to return this call. The parents phoned

twice. Something about a manual their son bought in the boys' room."

Hiccup's eyes grew wider, mirroring my own. From under my hand came a muffled *hic-hic*.

"What was that?" Goldie's mother said.

"What was what?"

"That chirping sound."

Hic-hic.

"There it is again. Coming from under my desk ..."

The high heels spiked closer.

"Mother—no! No!" Goldie babbled. "It's—it's be-hind the door. There's a bird behind the door!"

Hic-hic!

I pressed my lips against Hiccup's ear. "Think—*Mom*," I whispered.

At the magic word his eyes glazed over. *"Hic-aaaaah,"* he said, and his body relaxed.

"Don't be ridiculous, honey," the Principal said. "It must be my pager."

She hustled back toward the desk. Back toward *us*.

I hunched lower. Closed my eyes.

This is it, I thought.

"Mother—quick!" Goldie cried. "There's a huge girl-fight going on—right outside the window! Ooh! Ow! They're ripping out *hair* and everything!"

"Oh, dear." The Principal's shoes tap-tapped full-speed from the room. Goldie's sneakers slapped after her.

Silence.

"C'mon," I croaked. "Let's get out of here."

We unpretzeled ourselves from under the desk, and nearly fell trying to race through the door at the same time. I grabbed the copied coupons from the staff room. Then we charged out into the hall, nearly colliding with Goldie and her mother-the-Principal.

"But, Mother," Goldie was saying. "I could've sworn I saw a fight! Girls. Roving packs of hissing and spitting girls. With tattoos!"

"I think you need an appointment with the eye doctor," the Principal said. "May I help you, boys?"

"Uh, no—no, thanks," I said. "Just—just picking up some photocopies!"

"Photocopies," Hiccup agreed, nodding.

Goldie wiggled her eyebrows at me, as if to say: *Did you get the information?*

I shook my head and said, "Bye, Mrs. Laux. Keep up the good work!"

I felt Goldie's glare as Hiccup and I dashed out to the playground.

"Hoo-boy," I panted. "That was close. Too close."

"I—agree," Hiccup gasped. He leaned over, trying to catch his breath. "I almost—suffered—a myocardial—infarction."

"What's that?"

"Heart—attack."

"No way. You couldn't have."

Hands on his hips, he demanded, "Why not?"

"Because *I* was having one!"

Hiccup gaped at me. Then a slow grin crept over his face.

I grinned back.

The end-of-recess bell rang.

"We'd better go," I said.

"Yes," Hiccup advised. "At any moment we could be accosted by roving packs of girls. With tattoos."

That did it. We fell against each other, cracking up, then collapsed in a chortling heap on the grass. We laughed until our stomachs ached.

At last I sat up and wiped my eyes. "We're really late now. Come on."

We struggled to our feet and jogged slowly toward class.

"Hey," I said, not looking at him. "Um, I'm sorry about what I, uh, said last week. I didn't mean it. Honest."

Hiccup didn't answer, but he slowed to a walk.

"And, uh," I went on, "I'm sorry I didn't believe you were sick. But I would now."

Try looking up his symptoms sometime. It took some doing, but I'd finally found him. Right there on page 847 of Mom's medical book: *Hypochondria.* Which meant my friend had a sickness that made him worry all the time about being sick.

Now that I knew *what* was wrong with him, maybe someday I'd understand *why*.

Hiccup still didn't answer.

"And . . ." I said, filling the silence. "And I've missed—you know, hanging out with you and stuff."

"What about your new friends?" he asked.

I shook my head. "They're not my friends. They never were. They're not the kind of people who'll like you despite sneezes and . . . and hiccups. They only liked me because of my book. And when that fell apart..." My voice trailed off.

"I heard about the refund demands," Hiccup said. "Perhaps what your book needs is an illustrator. A talented person who could dramatize each bugging suggestion with an amusing cartoon."

I stopped in my tracks.

"I was thinking," Hiccup continued, "of a caped character similar to Medicine Man." He made the heralding sound of a trumpet. *"More irritating than a buzzing mosquito! Twice as annoying as hungry ants at a picnic! Able to pester parents with a single glance! He's a bother. He's a nuisance. He's—Bug Boy!"*

I laughed. "He's *perfect*. Will you really draw him for me? I mean—" my cheeks grew hot—"even after the things I said to you?"

"I will if you promise not to say them again," Hiccup answered. "And if you consent to splitting the profits."

"What! You want *half*? But that's not fair! The book was my idea."

He shrugged. "Take it or leave it."

I mulled it over. My friend was an excellent cartoonist. With his drawings my book would be twice as good. Four times as good.

"I'll take it," I said as we reached the door of the classroom. "But you've got to help me with the orders, starting today at noon."

"I would be happy to assist you," Hiccup said. "But I think it best that we move out of the boys' restroom. We need to reach a larger audience. The school parking lot should prove most fruitful."

"Hey, yeah. There'll be a ton of kids milling around out there, waiting for the bus or their parents. And we'll be ready!"

I glanced at him with admiration. "You know," I added, "for a sick kid, you sure don't have a very feeble mind."

Hiccup held my gaze. "You really think I'm sick?"

I nodded. "The sickest," I replied with a grin.

"Thank you," he said, and his face glowed.

"Say, look at this, Steve," Dad said from behind his morning newspaper a couple of days later. "There's an article here about a boy from your school."

"Mmm-hmpf," I answered, munching a mouthful of cereal. I wasn't really listening. Too busy mentally calculating how much money Hiccup and I had made since Tuesday.

Between Hayley's two-dollars-off coupon and Hic's idea to set up shop in the school parking lot, advance sales of my book had hit warp speed.

Plus, I'd sold almost every copy of the original List. Maybe fussy Pierre and his buddies wanted a "real" book. But the first graders were overjoyed at the idea of buying a simple list of bugging suggestions for the sale price of twenty-five cents. I'd even sold one to a curious mom!

Of course, I still needed a lot of money. Especially since I'd agreed to split my profits with Hiccup.

But I figured in another week I'd have made enough to pay for the book *and* the Invention Convention.

Dad chuckled, still reading the article. "This boy is causing quite a ruckus. Seems he's written a book for a class assignment and is selling copies of it on campus to his friends."

My hand froze in midair. Milk dripped off the spoon into my lap.

"Isn't that illegal?" Mom asked, automatically handing me a napkin.

"Yup," Dad said.

My mouth froze in midchew. Soggy corn flakes dribbled down my chin. Mom handed me another napkin.

"District policy," Dad went on. "No one can sell anything on campus, unless it's a school-sponsored project. But that's not the only problem this kid has caused. Says here that parents are bombarding the Principal's office with complaint letters and phone calls. One letter says: *Is this the type of behavior our schools are encouraging? Shame on the teacher who assigned this project! No wonder our country is suffering from moral decay!*"

Mom tsk-tsked. "Isn't that overreacting? I mean, what kind of book did this boy write?"

"It's called *101 Ways to Bug Your Parents*."

I choked.

"Oh, dear," Mom laughed, whacking me on the back. "What that boy's poor parents must be going through! Does it say who he is?"

Dad shook his head. "They're not releasing his name yet. The boy has a partner too and they're hoping to find out who he is today."

I leapt up. I had to get to school. *Now.* Hiccup was going to the doctor's at noon, so he'd volunteered to sell the books alone this morning. If the school knew about our parking lot sales, he'd be nabbed for sure....

I grabbed my pack and my lunch.

"These boys must be in your class, Steve," Mom said as I raced around the kitchen. "Do you know who they are?"

I opened my mouth, but only a squeak came out.

"Oh, my—look at the time!" Mom exclaimed. "I've got an experiment that has to be checked before eight. . . ." She balled up her napkin and hurried from the room.

Dad gulped the last of his coffee. "I'm late too," he said, and scooted after her.

Now was my chance.

Without saying good-bye, I charged out to the garage. No time for the bus today. I hopped on my bike, and with a running start pushed off into the street. I pedaled so fast, my feet must've been a blur. I careened around corners. Snaked through yards. Zoomed down alleys.

I had to get to Hiccup before anyone else did. It wasn't fair for him to take the fall for *my* project.

At last the school loomed in the distance. I spotted my friend sitting in our usual place in the parking lot, order forms spread out before him.

I skidded to a stop, spraying gravel.

"Hic—" I called, stumbling over my bike to reach him. "Hiccup!"

"HIC-HIC!" he answered. His eyes looked as sad as a lost dog's.

I followed his gaze to where a figure now stood behind me.

"Hello, Mr. Wyatt," Scribbler said. "We've been waiting for you."

NINETEEN

Hiccup and I watched, helpless, as Scribbler began to pick up order forms. He piled them neatly in a cardboard box.

"I'm afraid I have to shut down your business," he said, not looking at us. "And I have to hold on to these materials. I don't know for how long."

Gadabout coupons and copies of The List went on top of the order forms.

"But—but," I sputtered. "But you *can't*."

Scribbler shook his head. "You might want to think about choosing a new topic for your book. There's been considerable controversy about this. I'll back you up, but..."

I didn't hear the rest of his sentence. As the cash box disappeared into the carton, I heard only the sound of rattling coins. The sound of my canceled trip to the Convention.

So this was what Scribbler had meant by *or else*. I had promised him I would never bring another invention to school. Technically, I hadn't. But my book had caused as much trouble as all of my failed contraptions combined. Now Scribbler was determined that I face my punishment. He was taking away my book. Taking away my dream. . . .

Tears pricked my eyes.

The teacher folded the top flaps of the box. "I'm sorry, Mr. Wyatt," he said.

"You're not sorry!" My voice came out thick and bitter. "You've never liked me or any of my ideas! You were just waiting for an excuse to ruin this book. To ruin my future and—"

"*Sneeze,*" Hiccup pleaded. He glanced from me to Scribbler to me again, his eyes as round as two miniature full moons. "Sneeze, *please*—"

The teacher held up a hand. "It's all right, Mr. Denardo. He has a right to be angry. Let him say what he needs to. Go on, Mr. Wyatt."

"You—you—" I began.

But the words stuck in my throat. What was the point? Nothing I could say would save my book.

My anger deflated like an old party balloon.

"Oh, never mind." I looked down at the pavement, and scrubbed once at my eyes with a fist.

Scribbler stood silent for a long time. The first bell rang. Cars sputtered, doors slammed. Kids pushed past us in a blur, chattering, laughing, hurrying to class.

Finally, in a quiet voice, my teacher dropped the final bomb: "The Principal would like to see both of you in her office. Right away."

I shoved my fists into my pockets. "Not Hiccup," I

said. "This book was all my idea. He had nothing to do with it."

"That is inaccurate," Hiccup insisted. "We're (hic!) partners."

I stared Scribbler straight in the eye. He's *not* going."

"All right." The teacher nodded. "For now."

Hiccup plucked at my sleeve. "But (hic!), Sneeze—"

I pulled my thermos from my pack. "Take a sip, Hic. Everything will be okay," I said, although I knew it was a lie.

I trudged up the stairs toward the main entrance.

"Think of M.M.!" my friend called after me.

I glanced back. Medicine Man? What was he talking about?

Then I remembered.

I lifted my chin. Straightened my shoulders. Got ready to face the disease of injustice head-on.

"I'm sorry, Mr. Wyatt," Scribbler repeated, and his words sounded true. But I didn't answer. Didn't turn around. I just kept walking. . . .

The door to the Principal's office was closed. Two chairs stood guard on either side. One was empty. In the other lounged Ace.

"Hey," I said.

"Yo." He motioned for me to sit.

I perched on the edge of the other chair and cracked my knuckles.

"I heard," Ace said. "Tough break."

"You heard already?" I asked, incredulous. "Man, how do you know this stuff?"

Ace shrugged and arced one dark eyebrow. "I know."

I cracked another knuckle. "So what are *you* in for?"

"They finally found me out," he answered.

"Found you out ..." My imagination leap-frogged. Gang leader? Drug dealer? Chain-saw murderer?

I cleared my throat. "Uh, what exactly did you do?"

"I'm not supposed to be in class."

"What do you mean? Are you supposed to be in detention? Or—?"

Ace gave a luxurious cat stretch. "I'm not supposed to be in class. Period. I'm not enrolled in summer school."

No wonder I couldn't find his name in Scribbler's roll book!

"Then—then what were you doing here?" I asked.

"Hanging out."

"But why? Why Scribbler's class?"

Ace shrugged. "No place else to go."

"Ah," I said, as if I understood. But I didn't. I mean, Ace was cool. How could he not have someplace else, someplace *better*, to go?

And how could anyone be mean enough to turn him in?

"Scribbler," I said. "He found you out, and ratted on you, didn't he?"

Ace shook his head. "No. Scribbler's an okay guy. He knew all the time."

The door jerked opened. I heard the familiar tap-tap-tap-tap of high heels. Goldie's mother-the-Principal appeared, a green folder in her hand. "Smith?" she called. "John Smith?"

I glanced around. No one else in the reception area.

I started to say, "There's no Smith here," when Ace ambled toward her.

"Your real name is *John Smith*?" I blurted. "But—but—" My brain stumbled against the wacky names Goldie had conjured up. Tablespoonski. Shoppenoodle. "But it's so—*ordinary*!"

"Exactly," Ace said. He arced one dark eyebrow and gave me a knowing nod. The kind Clint Eastwood gives before he rides out of town at the end of a cowboy movie.

Then Ace sauntered into the Principal's office and shut the door.

I almost laughed. What a joke on Goldie! She'd be so disappointed!

Or would she?

. No, she'd find some way of using this *information* against him. And she'd make his life miserable. She'd start digging deeper and deeper into his life, trying to uncover his mysteriousness, until Ace wasn't Ace anymore....

Unless I didn't tell her.

And right then and there, I decided I wouldn't. Sure, maybe she'd hound me forever, insisting I still "owed" her. But I figured I owed Ace even more. That day in the bathroom he had saved my life.

Now we were even.

A few minutes later Mom soared into the reception area, her lab coat unbuttoned and flapping behind her like giant moth wings.

"Steve Wyatt, what is going on?" she demanded as soon as she saw me. "I got a call from Mrs. Laux insisting I come see her right away. I was in the middle of an experiment, but she said something about you selling stuff illegally on campus. You're not selling drugs, are you? Please tell me you're not selling drugs."

Just then Dad raced into the room, looking more rumpled than ever. His windblown hair stuck out all over, like Medusa's. "This better be good," he said, finger-combing the knots. "I had to cancel a class to be here. So what's going on?"

I sighed. "I'm the one who wrote the book."

"What are you talking about?" Mom said. "What book?"

"The one Dad was reading about this morning in the newspaper. *101 Ways to Bug Your Parents*."

"WHAT?" Mom and Dad roared.

I said meekly, "Why are you so mad? When you thought some other kid had written the book, you laughed. You thought the whole thing was funny."

"The key to that comment," Dad said with a frown, "is *some other kid*." Then a light of understanding brightened his face. "Oh, so that's what's been going on at home! You've been testing your research on *us*!"

"But what about drugs?" Mom asked. "I thought you were selling drugs."

I sighed. "No, Mom. I've been selling copies of the book."

"But *why*?"

"That's what we'd all like to know," said Mrs. Laux. She stood in the doorway, another green folder in her hand. "Good-bye, Ace," she called as he meandered past her. "I'll see you tomorrow morning. I've got a few errands you may run."

Ace flashed me a thumbs-up, then eased out the door.

"Stephen and Drs. Wyatt, won't you come in?" the Principal invited. She spiked her way into her office and motioned for us to sit down. I tried not to look at her desk, remembering with a shiver where I'd sat the last time I'd been in this room.

"Now," Mrs. Laux said, settling into her chair. "As I explained on the phone, we encourage our students to use their creativity in the writing class. However, there are a number of parents and community members who feel Stephen has acted *too* creatively. And that the school has acted irresponsibly by supporting his project."

She pointed to an inch-thick stack of papers on her desk. "These are the complaint letters and phone messages we've received in the last few days. A small, angry group of parents has called an emergency board meeting for this afternoon."

Mom and Dad exchanged glances. Then they looked at *me*. I looked down at my sneakers. The right one was untied.

"As you're probably aware," Mrs. Laux continued, "the Parents' Club funds our summer programs. If they decide the school is at fault, that we were wrong to allow Stephen to write this book, several things could happen.

"Staff members could be fired. Or the summer school programs could be cut from next year's budget. Or you, Stephen, could be asked to leave the writing class. Do you understand the seriousness of this?"

I swallowed against a lump in my throat, and nodded.

"You've been a bright, engaging student," the Principal went on. "Mr. Powell has spoken highly of your talents. But if we're going to support you, we need to know the 'why' behind what you've done."

"Well?" said Mom.

"Well?" said Dad.

"Well," I began.

And then I told them. About the Nice Alarm. The Convention. Mr. Patterson. And my dream.

"But why didn't you tell us all this before!" Mom said. "Times are tough, but we might've been able to do *something* to get you to the Convention. Or maybe we could've contacted this Mr. Patterson for you...."

Dad was nodding. "Yes, Son, absolutely. But you didn't tell us. *Why?*"

I shook my head. Not because I didn't have an answer. But because someone else had tried to get me to think about that question. To think about a why. But who?

Then I heard words parading inside my head: *What's the most important thing you're trying to say with this book? Why is this book so important to you?*

Scribbler. At the topic conference.

And that's when I knew there had been more than one reason why. It wasn't just the Nice Alarm. Or my future as an inventor. There was a deeper reason. Tucked away, cramped, hidden, but just as important.

I felt it unfold, stretch, reach out.

"I tried to tell you," I said at last, "but you never *listen*. I mean, you're so busy with school and the lab. You always have time for that stuff. But ... but not for other things. That's why I wrote the book...."

I took a deep breath. "So maybe you'd notice ... *me*."

TWENTY

O h!" Mom said. The word came out in a breath of quiet surprise, as if a kitten had leapt into her lap.

"*Oh,*" Dad said, with a blush in his voice. And I wondered if he was remembering the school of fish he'd sent swimming my way.

"It doesn't sound as if Stephen wrote the book with any malicious intent," Mrs. Laux observed. "That's a point in his favor."

"What does *malicious intent* mean?" I asked.

"You didn't purposely try to hurt anyone with your book, did you?" the Principal said.

I shook my head.

"And selling the books on campus. Did you know that was illegal?"

I shook my head again. "But," I added, "something told me the teachers wouldn't like it. That's why I took book orders in the bathroom."

"I see." Mrs. Laux jotted a few notes.

"What happens next?" Mom asked. "What happens to Steve?"

"And my book!" I blurted.

"As I mentioned earlier," the Principal reminded, "that will be decided this afternoon at the board meeting."

Dad took Mom's hand in his. "We'd like to attend."

"I was hoping you would. It's scheduled for two o'clock, in the auditorium."

"We'll be there," I said.

Mrs. Laux smiled. "I'm sorry, Stephen, but students aren't allowed at the meeting."

"But the meeting's about *me*. About my book. Shouldn't I be allowed to explain, to—"

"Someone will be speaking for you, Stephen. Please don't worry."

Mrs. Laux pushed back her chair and stood up. "Thank you for coming to see me on such short notice," she said, shaking hands with Mom and Dad. "Unless you have any other questions, Stephen may go to class and—"

"If it's all right with you," Mom put in, "we'd like to take Steve with us. I think we need a little time to talk."

"Of course," Mrs. Laux said. "See you this afternoon."

Dad steered me into the hall. I was glad for his steady hand on my shoulder. My legs felt wobbly.

"Let's take the convertible," he suggested. "We can throw Steve's bike in the trunk."

"All right," Mom said.

They didn't say another word the whole way to the parking lot. Where were they taking me? What would they do to me?

I climbed gingerly into the back of Dad's car. The leather, heated from the sun, burned through my jeans.

I was sitting in a hot seat. In more ways than one.

As Dad started the engine, I finally got up enough courage to ask, "So, um, are you guys still mad?"

Mom put on her sunglasses. "What do *you* think?"

"Well," I began, "I got a job without asking you. And, um, I never went to Hiccup's after school, like you told me to. Oh, yeah, and I made friends with a tattooed guy who—"

"Hold on, there," Mom said, twisting in her seat to look at me. "What's this about a job?"

"Oops." I gulped. "I guess I forgot to tell you about Gadabout Golf."

"I guess you're right," Dad said. He slowed the car and parked along a curb. "We've got plenty of time now. Maybe you'd like to tell us."

So I did.

Mom sighed. "Is there anything else you've forgotten to mention? Anything else we should know?"

"Let's see . . . Nice Alarm, Convention, Gadabout. No, I think that's about it. So . . . *are* you still mad?"

Dad tapped the steering wheel. "Mad isn't the word I'm looking for," he said. "I think we're more . . . *bugged*."

Mom laughed. "So your book works. And maybe we deserve it."

She tugged off her lab coat and tossed it on the backseat. Then she took off her sunglasses and stared, as if she hadn't really seen me in a long, long time.

"We haven't been much of a family the last couple of years," she said softly. "Your father and I—even you, Steve—we all have work that's important to us. Very important. But we need to be important to each other too. Maybe we forgot that along the way."

Dad nodded. "But that doesn't mean you're off the hook. You've pulled a few stunts that are unacceptable. The three of us will have to talk about your behavior. We can't let this happen again."

"Oh, it won't!" I promised.

"I'd like to make you a deal," Mom said. "You start talking to us—not bugging, but really *talking*—and I promise we'll start listening. With all ears. Starting this afternoon, right after the board meeting."

I grinned. "Is that this afternoon real time . . . or Mom time?"

Mom smoothed a windblown strand of my hair. "*Real* time," she answered, smiling back. "Give or take ten minutes."

"It's a deal," I said.

"Good." Dad started the car and pulled into traffic. "But for now, I think we need to have a little fun. Don't you?"

"Where are we going?" I asked.

He caught my gaze in the rearview mirror. "It's such a nice day," he said, humming a little, "I thought we'd play a game of miniature golf."

We played two games, and I won both by a landslide. Mom and Dad claimed I beat them only because I knew the ins and outs of the course. But the real reason was that, between the two of them, they lost five balls in the no-longer-scummy pond.

After the games we ate hot dogs and slurped sodas in the picnic area. Then I took my parents to the office to meet Mr. Barker.

"Why aren't you in summer school?" he boomed. "You're not sick are you?"

Dad draped an arm across my shoulders. "He's fine. We're just playing hookey today."

"What a relief," Mr. Barker said. "I can't afford for him to miss a single day. Your boy has done wonders for Gadabout. I could read you a list as long as a golf club of what he's fixed around here. And look at the customers." He motioned toward the course.

My mouth dropped open. "So *that's* why this place looks different today," I said. "There are *people* here. People playing golf!"

Mr. Barker chuckled. "Not exactly Grand Central Station yet. But business is picking up a bit . . . and all because of your coupons."

"Coupons?" Mom asked, looking puzzled.

"It's a long story," I answered.

"And it seems to be getting longer and longer," Dad said, but his laugh took the sting from his words.

Mom glanced at her watch. "It's late. I want to stop at home and change. And *you*," she said to me, "need to report to work."

"You mean," I said, "I can still work here?"

"I don't think Mr. Barker would have it any other way." She headed for the car. "Just make sure you're home by five-thirty. We'll have a lot to talk about after the board meeting."

The meeting. I'd forgotten.

Almost.

"I'm sorry you have to go to this meeting," I said as Dad took my bike from the trunk. "And I'm sorry I caused so much trouble. I—"

Dad shook his head. "Don't worry about that now, Son. And thanks for a fun morning."

"Yeah. It *was* fun, wasn't it? Maybe we can do it again sometime."

"Sure!" Dad agreed. "How about next Saturday?" With a wave, he revved the engine and drove off, passing Goldie and Hayley in the parking lot.

"So you *are* here," Goldie called, as if she couldn't believe her eyes.

She charged through the front gate and plopped down onto a picnic bench, fanning her face with her hands. "After what happened this morning, I thought for *sure* you'd be home in bed, buried under the covers. But Hayley said no way. She knew you'd be here, though I still don't know *why*. Something about inventing being what you *do*. Whatever *that* silliness means."

I smiled into Hayley's eyes. Funny, but they didn't seem so ice-cream cold anymore. Instead, they were the cool, clear blue of a summer sky.

Hayley tucked her hair behind one ear and smiled back. And I flashed on a thought: It doesn't matter as much now what happens at the board meeting. Not when I know there's one person who understands.

"Are you *listening*, Sneeze?" Goldie gabbed, tugging my sleeve. "I said, I just overheard my mother, the Principal, talking to Scribbler. And not only are *you* in trouble, but *he* is too! That's what we hurried here to tell you! Isn't that the best dirt you've heard all summer?"

"Why would Scribbler be in trouble?" I asked.

"Because he approved your book, of course!" Goldie rolled her eyes in exasperation. "And now there's a bunch of parents demanding he be fired.

Only Scribbler said there's no way he'll be fired. Because if the board makes you change your topic, he swears—" she paused for effect—"he swears *he'll quit!*"

I thunked onto the bench beside her. "I don't get it. Why is he sticking up for *me*? He's the one that ratted on me in the first place!"

Hayley shook her head. "No, he isn't. I guess you sold a copy of The List to a mom the other day. Mrs. Laux said the mom told a bunch of other parents, and got them writing nasty letters to the school and the newspaper and then—"

"So it *wasn't* Scribbler," I interrupted. "He wasn't trying to punish me after all...."

I jumped up. Checked my watch.

"See ya later!" I hurried out the gates to unlock my bike.

"Where are you going?" Goldie demanded.

"He's going to the board meeting," Hayley said. "Sneeze, put your bike away. Since there's no one here right now, I'll get my dad to drive us."

TWENTY·ONE

We were late.

The meeting had already started. Through the closed auditorium doors I could hear a battle of angry voices.

"Mr. Powell is setting a bad example. Teachers must be role models..."

"The book is inappropriate! And it's inappropriate for a teacher to support it!..."

"What will Mr. Powell encourage his students to write next? Books on robbing banks? Building bombs?..."

"But the book is funny...."

"Funny?! My son read it, and do you know what he said to me the other day? He said ..."

A gavel pounded once, twice, three times.

"Order! I must ask you to ... please ... one at a time!"

We opened the doors a slice to take a peek.

Goldie gave a low whistle. "Whoa, look at the crowd! And who are those guys jumping up and down! It's like they're on *Let's Make a Deal*."

Rows of parents and teachers were clotted close to

the stage. Most were sitting and listening with care. But a small group in front stood shaking their fists, mouths open, faces red. Onstage, five people sat behind a long desk. I guessed they were the board members. Mrs. Laux sat there too, her lips pinched, gavel in hand. She looked as if she were ready to hit someone with it.

"Go, Mother, go," Goldie murmured.

"Can you see your parents?" Hayley whispered.

I shook my head. "But I know they're here somewhere."

"Hey, there's Scribbler!" said Goldie.

Our teacher strode to a microphone set up at the front of the auditorium. He tapped it twice, then blew into it. "Excuse me!"

His amplified voice boom-echoed off the walls.

The audience quieted.

"As the boy's teacher," Scribbler said, "I would like to say a few words to the board."

Mrs. Laux nodded. "Please continue, Mr. Powell."

Scribbler adjusted his glasses and cleared his throat.

"I think this whole thing has been blown out of proportion," he began. "What Mr. Wyatt created is a simple list. A list of 101 things that children often do to bug their parents. Things I'm sure that *we* often did to bug our own parents."

Was that true? Somehow I couldn't imagine Scribbler—or even Mom and Dad—squirting milk out their noses.

"Now, some parents view this list as being not in the best of taste," Scribbler continued. "But it's certainly not harmful. I have rules in my classroom. No student—or teacher, for that matter—is allowed to say or do anything that could hurt or harm a fellow classmate. Mr. Wyatt knows this. And I think he understands why I've had to send home most of his inventions."

Goldie snickered, and my cheeks prickled hot. Which invention were she and Scribbler remembering?

Probably *all* of them.

"I knew I might catch flack for allowing Mr. Wyatt to write this book," the teacher said. "But it's students like him—inventive, creative discoverers—who grow up to be the movers and the shakers in this world. So we can't squash their ideas. We can't squash them into identical, cookie-cutter molds. Our job is to guide, to encourage. Otherwise, when they're older, they—"

I didn't hear the rest. I felt kinda dizzy. Giddy. Scribbler-the-Mighty-Invention-Hater had called me inventive. Creative. A discoverer. He was defending me. *Me.* The kid who'd melted his toupee. The kid who'd given him the glow-in-the-dark butt. The kid who...

The angry voices had clashed again, interrupting.

"The topic is still inappropriate for a school assignment!"

"That book encourages misbehavior. We have enough trouble controlling our children today without..."

"I recommend that Mr. Powell be asked to resign. We don't want teachers like him influencing our children and..."

"Resign!" I said through clenched teeth. "But—but that's not fair! The book wasn't *his* idea. Somebody—somebody should tell them."

"Well, don't just stand there," Goldie said, hands on her hips. "Go do it! That's what you came for, isn't it?"

I peeked through the door again. The small crowd in front reminded me of Pierre and his friends that day in the bathroom.

Scary. *Crazy.*

I glanced at Hayley and swallowed at the fear in my throat.

She pushed open the door. "We'll be right behind you," she said.

"*We?*" Goldie squeaked.

"Okay." I took a deep breath. "Here we go."

"*We?*" Goldie repeated.

Hayley caught her arm, dragging her after me down the aisle.

I tried not to look around at the people staring at

me. Instead I marched past row upon row of faces, focusing only on the microphone up front, and the way the metal glinted in the lights.

Scribbler had been shouted down. Out of the corner of my eye I could see him sitting in the front row. I took his place at the microphone. I could hear my breath amplified to sound like Darth Vader's. I could feel dozens of eyes boring into my back.

Uneasy, I turned. But instead of the eyes, I saw only Hayley. She was smiling. And looking at that smile was like looking into a mirror. I could see myself. And I could see that I was right.

If only Hiccup were here, I thought. He'd see the same thing too. Then I chuckled. No, he'd hate this. He'd be hiccupping so hard into the microphone, the hicks would sound like bullet ricochets. People would be screaming, ducking for cover...

The chuckle helped me relax. I tapped the microphone. "Uh, hello?" I said. "Hello?"

One of the board members said, "Who is this boy? Students are not allowed in these proceedings."

"I'm Sneeze—I mean, Stephen Wyatt," I said. "And I wrote the book you're talking about. So I think I should get to say something."

The audience buzzed. Before they could get out of hand again, Mrs. Laux banged her gavel.

"Go ahead, Stephen," she urged.

"I just wanted to say ... that I don't think it's right

for you to fire Scrib—Mr. Powell. I mean, this book was *my* idea, not his."

I heard parental voices grumbling behind me, but I ignored them. I didn't know any of the board members, so I went on, looking straight at Mrs. Laux.

"On the first day of class, Mr. Powell said that our best ideas come when we're writing about something that's important to us.

"I don't think Mr. Powell liked my idea for this book. But he asked me if I thought it was important. If I had a good reason for writing it. I told him yes. And I told him why. He thought I had a good reason. He okayed my topic. But he okayed it without knowing the whole story. I told him I was going to sell the book to make money. But I never told him *where* I was going to sell the book.

"So, if it's wrong for me to write this book *at school* . . . tell me, and I'll stop writing it here. If it's wrong for me to sell the book *at school* . . . tell me, and I'll stop selling it here. It's okay if you punish me. But *not* Mr. Powell."

Silence.

"Um, that's all I have to say. Thank you."

No one said a word. No one made a sound.

At last Mrs. Laux nodded. "Very well said, Stephen. Thank you."

I nodded back and turned around. Hayley was grinning like the Cheshire cat. Goldie was doing a great impression of my fish Ben, her mouth popping open and shut, with nothing coming out.

"Let's—go—" she managed to croak, "before—they—riot."

I moved to leave.

And that's when I heard the clapping.

Mr. Powell. Front and center. Mr. Powell—*clapping*.

Others slowly joined in. No one from the Let's-Make-a-Deal crowd clapped, but row upon row of other hands took up the beat, the sound swelling and roaring like a giant wave that rushed over us all and vibrated inside my chest.

Goldie, Hayley, and I rushed up the aisle, letting the tide carry us. I saw Mom and Dad as we flashed past. Mom's smile looked too big for her face. Dad waved.

The gavel pounded.

The applause died.

"I think we've heard from enough speakers today," Mrs. Laux announced. "The board would like a few minutes to discuss the issue, and then we'll make a decision."

The audience murmured and rustled, fidgeting in their seats or standing to stretch—but they didn't object.

The three of us stood at the door to wait. Mom and Dad squeezed through their row and hurried up the aisle.

"You were great, Son," Dad said.

Mom gave me a quick hug. Then she leaned over and whispered low in my ear, "We're very proud of you, Steve. It's your kind of initiative and drive that makes the difference between wannabe inventors ... and successful ones."

Hayley squeezed my hand. I don't know if she was trying to give or get support.

"How long do you think they'll take?" she asked.

"My mother, the Principal, is very efficient," Goldie said. "She'll hustle them along."

True to her daughter's word, ten minutes later Mrs. Laux pounded the gavel.

"The board has reached a decision," she announced. "Please take your seats."

A hush fell over the auditorium.

I crossed my fingers and toes. I would've crossed my eyes too, if I thought it would help.

"First," Mrs. Laux began, "since the class description set no guidelines as to what *kind* of books should be written by the students, we've decided that Mr. Powell is not in the wrong for allowing Stephen Wyatt to choose his own topic."

Goldie, Hayley, and I let out a cheer.

"Quiet!" the Principal said. "I'm not finished. Second, Stephen is free to continue writing his book, and will be allowed to display it at the library during Young Authors' Month."

Hayley and I slapped a quiet high five and whispered, "Yes!"

"However," Mrs. Laux said, "we would like to suggest that a disclaimer be included in the book, releasing the school—and the author—from all liability. That means, Stephen, that if your readers get punished for bugging their parents, they won't have grounds to sue you."

Whoa. I'd never thought of that. I made a mental note to write a disclaimer on the very first page.

"One last issue." The Principal sounded sad but firm. "The board finds it inappropriate for Stephen to continue printing his book on the school photocopier. It is also inappropriate for him to sell the book on school property. I'm sorry, Stephen, but you'll have to make other arrangements."

The small, angry crowd of parents mumbled and grumbled, their voices rising in argument.

Mrs. Laux banged her gavel. "The board's decision is final. Meeting adjourned."

A little cheer rose up around me. People reached out to shake my hand, clap me on the back, tousle my hair.

"What's wrong, Steve?" Mom asked, peering into my face. "Don't you understand? You've won!"

"And you saved Scribbler," Goldie said. "Though I'll never understand *why*."

"It's just that—" I stopped to swallow. "It's just that if

I can't sell the book on campus, I'm not sure I can sell enough copies in time. And if I have to photocopy the book at a print shop, that'll raise my expenses and ..."

The full meaning hit me in the stomach.

"I won't have enough money to go to the Invention Convention."

"Oh," Hayley said. She looked like she might cry. "And after all that work ..."

Dad squeezed my shoulder. "I'm sorry, Steve. You've gone through a lot to get to this Convention."

"I wish there was some way we could help, honey," Mom said. "Our money situation really is tight, but maybe—"

"Next year," Dad said in a firm voice. "I promise, Steve, we'll do everything we can to get you there next year."

Next year.

Next year would be too late!

Or would it?

I glanced at Hayley. She was squinting at me, and her squint was a challenge. She said, "You can build a lot of inventions in one year."

I shook my head, not understanding.

And then I remembered what I'd said to her the day she told me about her mom.

Inventing is what I do.

Okay, so I couldn't go to the Convention. Did that

mean I'd stop inventing? Just give up and cry and walk away?

No. Because inventing is who I am, and who I want to be. Always.

Sure, making money, being famous, and all that stuff is nice. But it's just icing on the cake.

Doing something because you enjoy it, because you believe in it, because it's *right*—that's what counts.

And the rest? Well, that would come later. I knew it. I knew I could make the Nice Alarm—and all my other inventions—a success. Maybe not this year. Or next year. Or the next.

But I would do it someday.

Because you *can* make dreams come true.

EPILOGUE

Hayley's story about her mom won first place at the library's Young Authors' Month awards. (She said she couldn't have done it without my helpful suggestions!)

101 Ways to Bug Your Parents got honorable mention. (And I couldn't have done it without hers.)

"Humph," Goldie said after the ceremony. "It's not fair. You guys got ribbons, savings bonds, *and* a handshake from the mayor. So what does the District Manager in charge of Special Orders and Purchasing get? The big zippo! And on top of that, Sneeze, you still owe me...*information*."

"Sorry, Goldie." I hid a smile. Ace's real name would go with me to my grave. "I'll pay you back somehow, someway, *some*day. I promise."

"You bet you will," she answered with a flip of her hair. "Because you owe me and you owe me big. And *I* know where you live."

After summer school ended, Hiccup and I split the money we'd earned on the book. Hic spent his half on a drawing table made especially for illustrators. I put mine in a savings account called "I've Got an Idea, Inc."

During the next year I built several new inventions, including the Golf Gopher and the Keep Kool Baseball Kap (the one with the mini sprinkler on top).

I also worked weekends with Hayley at Gadabout Golf. The two-dollars-off coupon helped pull in more customers, and the course actually started making money again—enough to really spruce up the place and get me a good raise.

Hayley even hired another girl to work the counter. "I need more free time for my writing," she admitted. "I mean, I love working here. But maybe Dad's right. Maybe there *is* life after golf."

Most of the money I made during the next year got socked away into my bank account, and by the following summer I'd saved five hundred dollars. Mom and Dad were so proud, they paid for all three of us to attend the Invention Convention.

There I finally met Mr. Sterling Patterson himself.

"I've got good news and bad news," he said.

The bad news was, he didn't much like the Nice Alarm. The good news: He liked my book. He liked it so much, he sent it to an editor friend at a major publishing house. The editor liked it too, and published it the following year.

101 Ways to Bug Your Parents was a hit.

Now I've got enough money to produce the Nice

Alarm myself. And the Keep Kool Baseball Kap. And the bubble gum that doesn't lose its flavor.

I've even got some clout at the publishing house and plan to put in a good word about Scribbler's book—if he ever finishes it.

And I finally got Goldie off my back.

"Here," I said, handing her a package the day my book hit the stores. "I promised you this a long time ago. Back when I first hired you as my District Manager in charge of Special Orders and Purchasing."

Goldie eyed the package with suspicion. "Is it a bomb?"

I laughed. "No, it's not a bomb."

"Well, what is it?"

"Open it."

She tore off the wrapping. "Oh, *cool*! A first edition of your book! Is—is this mine? To keep? Wow, thanks. But, hey—don't think you're off the hook. You still owe me information...*remember?*"

I shook my head. "No, I'd say we're about even now, Goldie. Take a look."

She opened to the title page and read:

101 Ways to Bug Your Parents
written by Stephen Wyatt
illustrated by Hector Denardo

"So what?" Goldie demanded. "I already know who you are."

"Keep going," I urged. "There . . . on the acknowledgments page."

Goldie read, "The author would like to thank the following people for helping with the research and writing of this book: Hiccup Denardo, Hayley Barker, Mr. Powell, my parents, and—" She gasped. Clutched the book to her chest. And smiled. An I've-never-been-happier smile.

"Oooh!" she cried. "Wait'll I tell my friends! They'll be *green* with envy!" She shoved the book back into my hands and dashed for the phone.

"You didn't slip a fifty-dollar bill in there, did you?" Hiccup asked.

"Nah," I said with a laugh. "I gave her what she's always wanted. Her name in lights."

I pointed to the final acknowledgment, which said:

. . . and to Goldie Laux, who knows 101 ways to drive me crazy.

---

101 WAYS TO BUG YOUR PARENTS

1. *Slurp your dinner.*
2. *Chew with your mouth open.*
3. *Burp with your mouth open.*
4. *Don't say: "Excuse me" after you burp.*
5. *Feed the dog/cat from the table.*
6. *Blow your nose at the table. Loudly.*
7. *When your dinner arrives, hold your nose and say: "Eww! What* smells*?!"*
8. *Blow bubbles in your milk.*
9. *Laugh with a mouthful of milk until some squirts out your nose.*
10. *Take one look at your plate, then say: "I'm not hungry." Later, ask for ice cream.*
11. *Use all the hot water in the shower.*
12. *Use all the toilet paper and don't put on a new roll.*
13. *Only brush your front teeth.*
14. *Don't brush at all—just wet your toothbrush.*
15. *Eat candy after you brush.*
16. *Wait until your mom's in the shower, then bang on the door and shout: "It's an emergency!"*

17. *Turn on the hot water when your dad's in the shower.*

18. *Fill the bathtub to the rim, then pretend there's a typhoon.*

19. *Don't flush.*

20. *Don't make your bed.*

21. *Leave half-eaten food under your bed. For weeks.*

22. *Read in the dark.*

23. *When it's time to go to bed, ask to stay up a half hour more. Then another. And another.*

24. *Don't get up on time.*

25. *Miss the bus so they have to drive you to school.*

26. *Take a nap instead of doing your homework.*

27. *Wake them up when they're sleeping in on weekends.*

28. *Turn on the TV really loud, then say: "I can't hear it."*

29. *Say: "Shut up" when they interrupt your favorite TV show.*

30. *Give your brother or sister a haircut.*

31. *Tease your brother or sister.*

32. *Blame everything on your brother or sister.*

33. *Bribe your brother or sister to do your homework and housework.*

34. *Make goofy faces during the family holiday photo.*

35. *Give them the silent treatment.*

36. *Repeat everything they say.*

37. *Ask for six-month advances on your allowance.*

38. *Ask: "What'd'ya bring me?" every day when they come home from work.*

39. *Never play with the toys they buy you.*

40. *Sell your toys.*

41. *Sell your brother's or sister's toys.*

42. *Sell your brother or sister.*

43. *Spend two hours opening your birthday presents, then say: "Is that all?"*

44. *Forget to write thank-you notes to your grandmother.*

45. *Say: "But everyone else's parents bought them one!"*

46. *Pretend to barf in the new car.*

47. *Lose french fries under the car seat.*

48. *Play with the car's automatic door locks and windows.*

49. *Ride with your feet out the window.*

50. *On a trip say: "I have to go to the bathroom" every ten minutes.*

51. *Alternate number fifty with "Are we there yet?"*

52. *At home say: "This place is boring. When can we go on vacation?"*

53. *On vacation say: "This place is boring. When can we go home?"*

54. *Forget to pack your toothbrush and clean underwear.*

55. *Beg for a dog/cat.*

56. *After they give you a dog/cat, don't feed it when it's your turn.*

57. *Pretend you don't notice when the dog/cat wets on the floor.*

58. *Leave the door open every time you go in and out of the house.*

59. *Don't help carry in the groceries.*

60. *Come in the house with muddy shoes. (Extra points if the floor is freshly mopped.)*

61. *Snap, crackle, and pop your bubble gum.*

62. *Leave chewed gum in the pockets of your dirty pants.*

63. *Put clean clothes back in the laundry hamper.*

64. *Throw your dirty clothes on the floor, not in the hamper.*

65. *Never change your underwear.*

66. *Wear jeans with holes in the knees.*

67. *Don't wear the new clothes they buy you.*

68. *Don't answer the phone or the door.*

69. *Say: "Huh?" a lot.*

70. *Leave wads of used Kleenex all over the house. Soggy wads.*

71. *Listen in on their phone conversations.*

72. *Say you don't have a book when it's time to do your homework.*

73. *Make them come to school to bring the homework you "forgot."*

74. *Do your homework, but don't turn it in.*

75. *Pretend the dog ate your homework.*

76. *Pretend your brother or sister ate your homework.*

77. *Ask them for help with your homework, then let them do it while you watch TV.*

78. *Beg them for things when they're too tired to say no.*

79. *Don't comb your hair.*

80. *Don't bathe.*

81. *Drink milk or juice directly from the carton.*

82. *Say to your mom: "That's not a woman's job."*

83. *Say to your mom: "That's a woman's job."*

84. *Say to your mom: "My teacher's almost as old as you!"*

85. *Call your mom* babe, toots, *or* chick.

86. *Call your dad* mac, buster, *or by his first name.*

87. *Offer to count or pull out their gray hairs.*

88. *Be rude to their friends.*

89. *Take home the school rat for the weekend.*

90. *Take home the school rat for the whole summer.*

91. *Hit the newspaper when they're reading it.*

92. *Put ketchup on yourself and pretend you're hurt.*

93. *Bring bugs into the house. Big ones.*

94. *Say: "I need a Halloween costume" fifteen minutes before you do.*

95. *Be gross things for Halloween.*

96. *Volunteer them to do things at school.*

97. *Don't tell them where you're going or when you'll be back or who you'll be with.*

98. *"Lose" your report card.*

99. *Say: "I'll be there in a minute." Then never go.*

100. *Record weird messages on the answering machine.*

101. *When you don't get your way, sulk, cry, whine, or say: "Please, please, please,* puh-leeeezzze?*"*